S0-AQM-802

LOVE AND LUCIA

Looking out they could see lights in the distance which seemed to mingle with the stars coming out in the sky overhead.

"It is so beautiful!" Lucia said.

There was silence. Then the Marquis said in a different voice from any she had heard before: "So are you, Lucia."

As she looked up in astonishment he put his arms round her and drew her close to him. Then while she trembled because she thought she was stepping into a dream, his lips came down on hers. . . .

Only when a century seemed to have passed and the Marquis raised his head did she say: "I . . . I . . . love you! I feel as if you have given me something so . . . magical . . . so perfect that there are . . . no words in which I can tell you how . . . wonderful it was."

The Marquis did not answer, but merely kissed her again, and to Lucia it was as if they were both standing in a dazzling light which came not from the sky, but from within themselves.

Light is . . . love, she thought. Then there was nothing else in the whole world but the Marquis, his arms, his lips and him. . . .

Bantam Books by Barbara Cartland
Ask your bookseller for the books you have missed

Barbara Cartland's Library of Love Series

Love
and
Lucia

Barbara Cartland

BANTAM BOOKS
TORONTO · NEW YORK · LONDON · SYDNEY

LOVE AND LUCIA
A Bantam Book / March 1983

All rights reserved.
Copyright © 1983 by Barbara Cartland.
This book may not be reproduced in whole or in part, by
mimeograph or any other means, without permission.
For information address: Bantam Books, Inc.

ISBN 0-553-23194-4

Published simultaneously in the United States and Canada

Bantam Books are published by Bantam Books, Inc. Its trademark, consisting of the words ''Bantam Books'' and the por-
trayal of a rooster is Registered in U.S. Patent and Trademark
Office and in other countries. Marca Registrada. Bantam
Books, Inc., 666 Fifth Avenue, New York, New York 10103.

PRINTED IN THE UNITED STATES OF AMERICA

O   0 9 8 7 6 5 4 3 2 1

Author's Note

When I was in Venice for Easter 1982, I was vividly aware of the light which differs from that of any other place I have visited, except Greece. It is a particularly clear light and has an intensity that is mysterious and enchanting.

Venice is a dream city, and every time one goes there it is more beautiful than one remembered it to be.

This time I was entranced by the soft mist over the water first thing in the morning, the sun glittering on the mosaics outside San Marco, and the candles flickering inside. I was also entranced by the candles in the magnificent Banquetting Hall of the Palazzo Contarini Polignac when the *Duc* Decazes gave a dinner-party.

Will Venice survive? For ever and always in the hearts of those who love her.

Chapter One

1824

The Marquis of Wynchcombe awoke slowly and thought the heat was oppressive.

Then he realised that what he was noticing was the stuffiness of the room because the shutters were closed and the curtains drawn.

Almost as if he asked himself the reason for it, he turned sideways on his pillow and saw the answer beside him.

When he slept alone he invariably opened the windows last thing at night, and instead of enjoying the darkness of the shutters, he liked to see the first glimmer of the dawn creeping up the sky.

But his amusement of the night before was lying beside him, and hearing her soft breathing he knew that she was fast asleep.

He turned away from her, thinking with a faint smile on his rather hard lips that last night had been fiery and unrestrained, which was what he had expected from a Venetian, but, although he had no wish to admit it, it had also been somewhat exhausting.

He had known as soon as he heard Francesca Rosso sing that she had a voice like a nightingale, and her top notes soared like larks into the sun.

1

At the same time, she was young, beautiful, and apparently only too eager to be swept into his arms and under his protection.

The Marquis was very fastidious and exceedingly particular in bestowing his favours, but he had learnt almost as soon as he arrived in Venice who the most attractive women were, and in the theatrical world Francesca had no equal.

When she sang in the Opera there was not an empty seat in the house, and her praises were extolled with an eloquence that only the Italians can express, with their words, their hands, and their eyes.

After a long voyage from England, the Marquis was looking for amusement.

It was therefore only a matter of days before he met Francesca, and the moment she saw him she knew that if she was what he was looking for, she could return the compliment.

Since the occupation of Venice by Napoleon as King of Italy, the Venetians had grown increasingly poorer year by year.

The ancient families were struggling to remain alive and had little money to expend on the delights and extravagances which were part of their history. So, to the Courtesans of Venice, a rich English nobleman was a gift from the gods.

When, by the Congress of Vienna and the Treaty of Paris, Venice was ceded to Austria, things from the Venetian point of view were little changed.

The difference was simply that there was another Emperor in control, now in Vienna, and a Viceroy of a different nationality.

However they behaved, the Venetians loathed the Austrians, and the Marquis had yet to meet any Venetian who did not immediately start to abuse the Austrians and become boringly verbose on the subject of the insults and humiliations they received.

As far as he was concerned, he had come to Venice for pleasure.

After being unable to leave England for so many years, except to fight against Napoleon, English men and women were pouring out of the country in the tens of thousands to discover Europe.

The "Grand Tour" had almost totally changed its character. The means of travel now being easier and more comfortable, not only the aristocrats and monied people of the middle-class were the travellers, but also there were poets, writers, musicians, and painters, the latter gravitating towards Venice as if to a magnet.

The Marquis had met William Turner, who had spent a fortnight in Venice in 1819, and had listened to his paean of praise for what had been to him a revelation of light.

But while the Marquis was a notable collector of paintings to add to those which filled the large Picture Galleries both in his house in the country and in that in London, in Venice he was actually looking for something warmer and more human than a painting.

He certainly found it in Francesca.

From the moment she had moved into the exquisite *Palazzo* he occupied on the Grand Canal, he found himself amused and entertained in a way which made him applaud his decision to visit Venice.

The *Beau Monde*, he found, had altered in character now that the King, recently crowned, was older.

The parties His Majesty gave at Buckingham Palace and at the Royal Pavilion at Brighton were not the same as those which had enlivened, entertained, and scandalised a lot of people when he was the Prince Regent.

"Either they have become boring," the Marquis had said to some of his friends, "or else I am more easily bored."

They had laughed, and only Lord Duncan, his constant companion, had been brave enough to say:

"Both those assertions are correct, Giles. In fact,

3

no-one would dispute that you are growing more particular, more blasé, and certainly more cynical than you were five years ago."

Because people seldom spoke like that to the Marquis, he had looked at his friend in surprise before he had said:

"Perhaps you are right, but it is certainly a dismal portent for the future."

Alastair Duncan had laughed.

"With your money, Giles, there are always 'pastures new.'"

It was perhaps this remark which had made the Marquis start thinking that what he was doing, and had been doing during the years since the war had ended, had become monotonous.

It was not only the parties which were "much of a muchness," but the race-meetings, the Mills, the Steeple-Chases in which he took part, and in particular the women who, when he thought about it, lacked variety.

He was not yet so cynical as to say even to himself that all women, like cats, were grey in the dark!

But when he thought about it, his *affaires de coeur,* which followed one after another, seemed to tread the same path of exploration and satisfaction.

But after they reached a certain height they always fell precipitately into an oblivion for no reason which the Marquis could ascertain, except that he was bored.

It was Alastair Duncan who spelt it out for him the last evening before he left London.

"Have you ever asked yourself, Giles," he enquired, "what you are looking for, or rather aiming for, in life?"

The Marquis, who had enjoyed a superlative dinner supplied by his French Chef, was sitting back with a glass of brandy in his hand, and replied:

"Why should I be looking for anything?"

"Because you cannot help it," Alastair replied.

"I have no conception of what you are talking about."

"Then listen to me. You are one of the wealthiest men in the country, you are certainly the most handsome, the most athletic, and, although you seldom consider it, one of the most intelligent. In those circumstances it must be impossible for you to be content as you are now."

"Nonsense!" the Marquis said positively. "I am of course flattered by your description of me, but I assure you I am extremely content with my possessions, my position in life, and certainly my horses."

"And you really think they are enough to occupy you and engage your mind for the next forty or fifty years?"

The Marquis laughed.

"Why not?"

"You are being obtuse," Alastair said, "or else dishonest with yourself, which is something I have never known you to be before."

"What the devil are you driving at?" the Marquis enquired.

"I think the answer to that is that it makes me sad to see anything so exceptional as you being wasted."

"In what way?"

Now there was a slight edge to the Marquis's voice.

"I think perhaps it is because you are, as you say, content. But I find it impossible to believe that anybody with brains could be content with the people with whom you spend your time at the moment."

"What is wrong with them?" the Marquis asked sharply.

"Take the King, for instance," Alastair replied. "We all like 'Prinny,' we always have, but he has grown increasingly fat, slow, and, if we are honest with ourselves, tedious."

The Marquis's eyes twinkled, but he did not interrupt as Alastair went on:

"Ever since he has been besotted by one fat, elderly, avaricious woman after another, I find it hard to concentrate on what he is saying. I only feel increasingly eager to escape from the Royal Presence as quickly as possible."

As he finished speaking Lord Duncan waited, as if expecting the Marquis to contradict what he had said, but he merely took a sip of brandy and remarked:

"Go on, I am interested."

"Do you want me to go through the whole collection of 'hangers-on' and spongers, male and female, who fawn upon you because you are rich, and because there is nobody else at the moment who can provide them so ably with what they desire?"

"What is that?" the Marquis asked.

"Hospitality, amusement, and the feeling that if you are there, they are in the right place."

The Marquis threw back his head and laughed.

"I have never known you to be so eloquent, Alastair, or so perceptive. I thought that when we did things together you enjoyed yourself."

"I do, you know I do!" Alastair replied. "At the same time, I am very much aware that you do not enjoy life as much as you used to when we were suffering the discomforts and hardships of being in the Army, and yet were young and enthusiastic enough to enjoy it."

"We all have to grow older," the Marquis said philosophically.

Alastair Duncan laughed.

"You talk as if you were Methusala. You will be thirty-four next birthday, and there is still, or there should be, a little 'life in the old dog yet'!"

The Marquis rose to his feet.

"Come now, Alastair, I do not know what you are getting at, but it is making me uncomfortably introspective."

"That is what I hoped, and I am also telling you why I am glad you are going away."

"All right, I am going away because I am bored," the Marquis conceded. "I am quite certain, however, that by the time I reach Venice I shall be only too glad to turn round and come straight back again."

"I shall be waiting to welcome you with open arms," Alastair said. "I only wish to God I could come with you!"

"Chuck the Army and do so," the Marquis suggested. His friend shook his head.

"No, I thought about leaving the Army when peace was declared, but I decided that until my father dies, as I have no Estates to care for, as you do, I should have some occupation to fill my days rather than going from Club to Club, party to party, and bed to bed!"

The Marquis laughed again.

"I commend you, Alastair, for your decision, your way of life, and your criticism of mine. At the same time, damn you for your impertinence!"

Only when he had set off the following day, with a large entourage to see to his comfort, did the Marquis remember what his friend had said, and admit that there was some truth in it.

But what was the alternative, he asked, except to win more races than he had won already, to ensure that his Estates were in perfect running order, and to dance attendance on the Monarch because the King demanded it of him?

"What do you want to go abroad for?" he had growled disagreeably when the Marquis had said good-bye to him.

Having, as Alastair might have said, played nursemaid to the impulsive, emotional Prince of Wales and the frustrated and often hysterical Prince Regent, the Marquis knew how to handle the new King.

"I know, Sire, it is something Your Majesty would do if it were possible for you," he said. "I see it as my duty to find out what is happening in different parts of Europe after the way the people have suffered under the heel of Napoleon."

"I imagine they can help themselves," the King replied.

"Not without our understanding, our help, and our inspiration," the Marquis answered.

He saw that the King was impressed, and added:

"Having won the war, Sire, it is our duty, as you yourself have often averred, to build and sustain the peace."

After this the King had bidden him God Speed in a different tone of voice, but at the same time he had said, and it was an order:

"Do not stay away for too long! I shall miss you, and I want you with me."

When the Marquis left the Palace he felt that he was escaping to a new freedom which he had not enjoyed for some years.

At the same time, he had not been optimistic that new interests abroad would engage his mind very much more fully than it was engaged in England.

Various of his friends had talked so much about Venice that he decided he would go there first and make it his main objective.

He therefore travelled through France to inspect the ravages of war, sending his yacht ahead so that it could be waiting for him when he arrived in Marseilles.

The journey did not interest him particularly, except for an amusing week in Paris.

In fact, he found the sunshine of the Mediterranean and the enjoyment of trying out his new "plaything" in the shape of his yacht, *The Sea Horse,* more to his liking.

Although he regretted to some extent that he was not accompanied by Alastair or some of his other friends, he had learnt in the past that a party was constraining and that even the most congenial people began to pall if one saw too much of them.

"I am better off on my own," the Marquis said to himself.

He found that that assumption was particularly true when he reached Venice.

He had sent his secretary ahead of him with a very experienced Courier to rent a *Palazzo* where at least he would be housed in comfort.

People who had returned from visiting Venice had said there were a large number of *Palazzos* available, belonging to Venetian aristocrats who were only too glad to receive a large rent for Palaces which they themselves found increasingly expensive to maintain.

The *Palazzo* which the Marquis found waiting for him on arrival was certainly impressive.

It had belonged to the same family for five generations, but the present owners were willing to move into very much smaller and cheaper premises while the Marquis was their tenant.

Although parts of the building were undoubtedly shabby and in need of repair, he was impressed by the excellent taste with which the ancient furnishings had been chosen.

Also, the large number of servants whom his secretary had engaged on his behalf soon gave the place the perfection the Marquis expected wherever he stayed.

In the dimness of the huge room in which he was now, he could see under the beamed and painted ceiling the heavy brocade curtains which covered the long windows and reached from ceiling to floor.

The same brocade draped the large bed in which he was lying, and which was surmounted by a carved and gilded canopy like that which stood above the Doge's chair, and made anybody lying beneath it feel important.

Then, as if the lack of air and the somewhat pungent perfume which came from Francesca's hair was too much for him, the Marquis very quietly slipped out of bed.

He walked across the room and into an adjacent one in which his valet had hung his clothes.

As he closed the door behind him he drew in a deep breath, as if searching for fresh air.

Then, after stretching himself and flexing his muscles in a manner which betrayed his strength, he washed in cold water before he began to dress.

At the moment he had no wish to summon his valet or any other servant. He just wished to be alone.

Perhaps the saturation of a long night of love-making, or perhaps the pale sun creeping up the sky and dispersing the haze which hung over the Grand Canal outside, made him want silence.

Ever since he had come to Venice he had been fêted, entertained, and, he thought now, encroached upon by people.

Now all he wanted was to escape and be by himself.

Because he was used to being self-sufficient, the Marquis dressed himself and tied his cravat as skilfully and as quickly as if he were being helped by a valet.

He had long ago made up his mind that anything a servant could do, he would do better.

Although he seldom put it to the test, he knew a feeling of satisfaction that no amount of help could have ensured his being dressed more quickly than he was at this moment.

It was still very early in the morning, and although perhaps the servants were stirring in the kitchen, there was no-one in sight as he walked from his dressing-room.

He descended the wide staircase which led to the lower part of the *Palazzo* and finally to the entrance to the Grand Canal, which in the winter was often flooded.

However, the Marquis did not go to the front of the *Palazzo*, where his private gondola was waiting.

Instead, he let himself out at the back onto a narrow passage between high houses, most of them still shuttered and barred.

The passage itself was empty, and only when he had walked a little way and come to a bridge did he look over the small canal beneath him and see a man leisurely propelling a gondola heaped with vegetables and fruit.

He knew he was on his way to the morning market, where most of the food consumed by the City was brought in from the countryside.

He walked on, and now the sun was sweeping away the last mists from the water, and as it did so, it created the translucent light which Turner had found so irresistible that he had tried to immortalise it on canvass.

However, at the moment the Marquis was thinking not of the exquisite architecture or the fusion of man-made and natural beauty, but of himself.

He had been in Venice for ten days and was already wondering, although it seemed absurd, how soon he should leave.

Francesca was certainly an inducement to stay, but although she attracted and excited him, he was already beginning to think it would be a mistake to let her become anything but dispensable.

It was almost as if he wanted to need her, to regret leaving her, and yet to go while he would still wish to stay.

"Alastair was wrong," he told himself as he walked on. "I have learnt nothing on this trip except that I prefer riding to walking, and the English to foreigners!"

Then he told himself that he was being reprehensibly insular, which was something he should not feel, but rather should have a child-like appreciation of everything that was new and different.

And yet, was it so different?

What of the conversations he had listened to at the dinner-parties that had been given in his honour?

· Were they not very much the same as what he had heard round his own table in Berkeley Square, or in White's Club?

And was not Francesca, when it came down to facts, very much the same as the "Incomparables" who threw themselves into his arms in London, or the Society Beauties who enticed him with an invitation in their eyes and a provocative pout of their lips?

"What do I want? What the hell am I looking for?" the Marquis asked, and found to his surprise that he was already in the Piazza San Marco.

He had walked quickly along the narrow *calletes* behind the Palaces, over the bridges which spanned the small canals, automatically going up the steps on one side of them and down the steps on the other.

He had been so deeply in his thoughts that he had reached the end of his walk almost before he was aware he had started it.

Now in the Piazza San Marco there were people, women and men hurrying to work or to the markets, and a few well-dressed gentlemen, coming either from a Casino or from a warm bed, on their way back to their own houses.

Others, like the Marquis himself, were walking across the great Square for exercise or in search of coffee in one of the Cafés which were to be found under the arches on either side of it.

The Marquis hardly looked at them, for at the moment he was no more interested in them than in the noble proportions of the buildings forming the sides of the *Piazza*.

The heels of his Hessian boots seemed to echo as he walked between the pillars and down two steps onto the pavement.

Facing the San Marco with its blaze of gold mosaics, its four superb bronze horses set above the central door, and its bubbling cupolas, he walked into the centre of the *Piazza*.

The pigeons strutted ahead of him, and then when he seemed to move quicker than they did, took to their wings and flew with a flutter a few feet farther on.

It was then that the Marquis saw the waiters putting the tables and chairs into place outside a Café and decided to have a cup of coffee.

Now that he thought about it, his mouth felt dry, either from the wines he had consumed the night before or, what was more likely, from the airlessness of his bed-chamber.

Unhurriedly he sat down at a table, having a wide choice at such an early hour of the morning, and instantly a waiter came for his order.

He gave it in Italian, knowing enough of the language

to make himself understood, even though he could not converse at any length.

Then he surveyed the beauty of the *Piazza* without really taking it in.

He was still thinking about himself, of what he should do, and whether in his own interests he would be wisest to return to London if not next week then certainly the week after that.

He could of course visit Naples or Rome, but he had no particular desire to do so, and he felt that it might prove even more boring than returning to what Alastair had called the "monotony of England."

The waiter brought his coffee and he poured it out, and as he did so he realised that he had chosen Florian's, the oldest Café in Venice, having been opened as long ago as 1702.

Now that he thought of it, he remembered that Venice's hostility to her enemies and new overlords was exemplified at the *Piazza*.

The Venetians frequented Florian's and boycotted Quadri's, which was patronised by the Austrians.

Where an Austrian Band played, no Venetian ever applauded, and they never looked in the direction of the flagpole in front of the San Marco, which carried the Austrian flag bearing the double-headed eagle.

It was this attitude, the Marquis thought, which made Venice so endearing, like a petulant child who continues to rebel however severely it has been punished.

Then as the sunshine increased and the San Marco seemed to dazzle almost blindingly behind the flag which to the Venetians was a continual reminder of their humiliation, he became aware that somebody was standing at his side.

Without even turning his head, he assumed it was a beggar and merely made a gesture of dismissal with his hand.

It was impossible to sit for any length of time at

Florian's or any other Café without being pestered for money or having something offered for sale.

This was traditional, and it was at Florian's that Guardi had attempted to sell his paintings before he became famous.

As whoever was opportuning him did not go away, the Marquis turned his head slowly, wondering if he had a small coin in his pocket to ensure his peace.

He then saw it was a woman who was standing by his table.

She was very slight, and he supposed she was in fact a beggar, until to his surprise she said in English:

"May I speak to you, My Lord?"

Her voice was quiet and well educated, and the Marquis saw that although she wore a shawl of some black material over her head, she was not in fact the sort of beggar he had expected.

As he looked a little more carefully at her, he saw that her face was dominated by her eyes, which were very large and were not blue, as he had somehow expected from her English voice, but the grey of the pigeons strutting about on the *Piazza*.

"You are English!" he exclaimed.

"I am English . . . My Lord, and as an English-woman . . . I need your help . . . desperately!"

There was no doubt that her clothes were poor and, the Marquis suspected, threadbare, but her voice was too cultured to belong to anyone but a Lady.

With somewhat of an effort he rose a little from his seat to say:

"Will you sit down, and tell me how I can be of assistance?"

Even as he did so, he thought that he was making a mistake. He would doubtless be regaled with a hard-luck story, and it would have been far easier to have given her money and told her to go away.

Then as she seated herself he saw that her features

14

were perfect, and her small straight nose could not have belonged to anybody who was not of gentle birth.

Her hands, too, while they were ungloved, which was unconventional, had long, slim, pointed fingers, and were, the Marquis noted with his critical faculty for detail, spotlessly clean.

She was looking not at him but away from him, and he had the idea that she was feeling for words and at the same time was shy.

It was not the attitude he would have expected of a beggar, and he said in a rather more gentle voice than he would otherwise have used:

"I am waiting for you to tell me what you wish me to hear."

Quite unexpectedly there was a smile on her lips as she said:

"The truth is, My Lord, I was so . . . certain that you would not listen to me, that now that you are doing so . . . I feel . . . overwhelmed."

"Why were you certain that I would do anything else?" the Marquis enquired curiously.

"Because none of the gentlemen I have approached here so far have done anything but tell me to . . . go away."

She gave a little sigh that seemed to come from the very depths of her being as she said:

"I am sure it is my fault, and I am not a good sales-woman. Nor is my father . . . which is the whole . . . trouble."

She paused, and the Marquis said:

"Suppose you start at the beginning? I am finding what you are saying somewhat hard to follow. Why are you in Venice when you are English? Are you a tourist, or do you live here?"

"We are living here, My Lord, and my father is a painter."

The Marquis smiled.

"Now I understand. It is his paintings which you have been trying to sell."

It was the old story, he thought.

Painters who had to live by what they produced invariably found it hard to find customers.

As Venice was stuffed with paintings by the greatest artists in the world, he could not imagine there were many casual purchasers to be found sitting in the Cafés of the Piazza San Marco.

As if she followed what he was thinking, the woman beside him said:

"We managed until Papa became ill, but now that he can no longer paint, I have to sell one of his paintings . . . if we are not to die of . . . starvation."

The Marquis looked at her sharply to see if she was exaggerating and making a good story in order to extract money from him.

But as he looked into her eyes he thought it would be impossible for anybody to lie and for what had been called the "windows of the soul" not to reflect it.

Her eyes were certainly different from those of any other woman he had ever seen before, in that they were as transparent as a stream.

He felt that he could see in them her anxiety that he would not listen to her and her fear that he might send her away.

Because he somehow wished to reassure her, he said:

"Is your father English, and is he perhaps better known in England than he is here?"

"I doubt if you will have heard of Papa," the girl answered, "but if you would, My Lord, just come and see his paintings, you would understand that while he paints in a very different manner from what is the traditional style in this City, he is, although I say it, a real artist."

The Marquis thought a little cynically that this was the sort of story he had often heard before, and he was wondering what he should reply, when the waiter stood at their table.

"Coffee for the *Signorina*?" he questioned.

"Yes, of course," the Marquis replied in Italian, and said to the girl beside him: "I am sure you would like a cup of coffee?"

He thought there was a sudden light in her eyes as she replied:

"I would . . . not wish to . . . impose on you, My Lord."

"I can afford it," the Marquis said with a faint smile.

"I know . . . that."

It suddenly struck him that she had addressed him as "My Lord," and he thought it had not been the ordinary flattery of a beggar to whom every English gentleman was a Lord, as a term of ingratiation.

As if she was aware what he was thinking, she explained:

"When I heard you had . . . come to Venice, I wondered if there would be any . . . chance of Papa approaching you to . . . look at his paintings. I have heard of your . . . collection in England, and Papa has often . . . talked of the Van Dycks you have at . . . Wynch, in Buckinghamshire."

The Marquis looked at her in surprise, but he did not speak, and she went on:

"I therefore thought you would . . . understand . . . as other people do not, what Papa is trying to . . . convey by his . . . painting."

She made a little gesture with her hands which was somehow very pathetic as she said:

"To me they are very beautiful . . . but they are not saleable."

"And so you have no money," the Marquis said, and felt it was a somewhat brutal statement of fact.

"Papa is ill," the girl replied, "and unless I can find some money, he will . . . die from lack of food more than . . . anything else."

She spoke quite simply in the quiet voice that the Marquis knew came from an iron self-control.

At the same time, because he was watching her eyes, he knew that she was longing to throw herself at his feet and plead with him to save them.

17

He was not certain how he knew this, and yet it was palpably clear to him that she knew it would be the wrong way to approach him and that only by stating her case calmly and quietly would he listen.

"What is your name?" he asked.

"Lucia Beaumont," she replied, "and my father paints under his own name, which is Bernard Beaumont."

The Marquis thought the name was too English for it to appeal to the type of collector who would think an artist from a foreign country must have a fancy name to be authentic.

As if she read his thoughts Lucia said:

"Mama used to say sometimes that Papa would get more attention as a painter if he signed his paintings as a Venetian or an Italian, but he is too proud to be . . . anything but . . . himself."

The waiter brought the coffee and put it down on the table.

Lucia looked at it, and the Marquis had the impression that because she was very eager to drink it she deliberately paused, keeping her hands in her lap, before she poured it slowly and very gracefully from the jug into the cup.

Then, still as if she was playing a part, she turned to give him a little smile before she said:

"Thank you for giving me . . . coffee. It is the first time anybody has offered me . . . coffee when I have . . . come here."

Now her smile faded and the little shudder she gave told the Marquis that what in fact had been offered was an unpleasant experience which she did not want to remember.

Then as he watched her sip the coffee, he said:

"Supposing you sell one of your father's paintings? What will you do then?"

"I will try to make him stronger," Lucia answered, "and if we can make enough money . . . return to England."

There was a little pause before the last three words, and the Marquis asked:

"Is that something you wish to do?"

"I think it is something we must do . . . even though it will be difficult."

"Why difficult?"

There was silence, and he knew she was wondering whether she could tell him the truth.

"I asked you," he said at length, "why it would be difficult for you to go back to England."

"There are reasons why it would perhaps be a mistake," Lucia said, "and yet, if anything happens to Papa . . . I would be very frightened to be here alone in this . . . strange country."

The way she spoke told the Marquis that it was a very real fear, and he tried to form a question which would not seem too inquisitive but would at the same time tell him what he wished to know.

Then as she finished her coffee Lucia said:

"It seems a great deal to ask Your Lordship . . . but could you come and look at Papa's paintings? It is not far from here, and although you may think it an . . . imposition to ask you, they are too big for me to bring for your . . . inspection without causing a . . . great deal of comment."

Now the anxiety and fear were back in her eyes, and it flashed through the Marquis's mind that it would be far easier to give her some money to go away.

He was quite certain that five pounds or even less in Venetian currency would keep her and her father at least from starvation for a week or so.

Then he told himself that it would be infuriating not to know the end of the story.

Perhaps she was just a trickster, a beggar who had thought up a tale that would prove irresistible when it came to extorting coins from a man's pocket.

Perhaps like other beggars she was just the enticer, the actor for those who were the brains behind the scheme of a pathetic young girl trying to save her father's life.

Then the Marquis told himself he was not so easily deceived.

19

He had dealt with men in the Army and had always known when they were lying to him.

He employed a great number of people on his Estates and relied invariably on his instinct where they were concerned rather than on what he was told about them.

In this case he was sure that Lucia was not putting on an act just to impress him, but was telling him the truth, and even while she did so she was praying that he would believe her.

He glanced down and saw that her hands were clenched so tightly together in her lap that her fingers were white with the pressure she was exerting on them.

He knew that, having got so far, she was terrified that he would now turn her away and have nothing more to do with her.

The Marquis drew some money from his pocket and put it down on the table, then rose slowly to his feet.

"Can we walk to where you are living?" he asked. "Or would it be better to take a gondola?"

As the light came into her eyes he thought that it seemed to eclipse the sunshine.

"You will . . . come? You . . . really will?"

"It is what you have asked me to do."

She gave a sigh that seemed to come from the very depths of her being.

"How can you be so kind and so very different from what I expected?"

The Marquis raised his eye-brows.

"What did you expect?"

"That you would be far too grand and important to bother with . . . beggars or impecunious . . . painters."

"And yet you were aware that I am interested in paintings."

She was silent for a moment. Then as she knew he was waiting for her reply, she said in a tremulous little voice:

"Paintings mean . . . different things to . . . different people."

"I understand what you are saying," the Marquis said, "and because that is undeniably true, I am curious to see how your father paints."

As he spoke he started to walk away from the Café, in the direction of the San Marco, and as she moved beside him he wondered how he had known that where she was living was not in the direction from which he had come.

Then as they walked across the centre of the *Piazza* with the pigeons fluttering ahead, the Marquis felt as if they were leading him.

Although his logical mind told him it was impossible, he knew he was on the point of discovering something new.

Chapter Two

The Marquis walked with Lucia along a narrow street from the corner of the San Marco, then into a much narrower *callete* in which the high houses on either side were in a very dilapidated condition.

It was what the Marquis expected.

At the same time, it struck him that if he was walking into a trap where he would be robbed and doubtless rendered unconscious, he had nobody to blame but himself.

Then Lucia led the way through a high double door of a Seventh Century building which the Marquis guessed had once been a nobleman's house.

There was a long flight of stone stairs winding upwards, and the steps themselves were chipped and broken.

As they climbed and went on climbing, the Marquis was glad that he was in good athletic condition.

He noticed that the steepness and height of the stairs did not seem to affect Lucia, and they moved side by side in silence until they reached the top landing.

From there the Marquis glimpsed through a small window a magnificent view over the roofs of the City.

Lucia opened a low door, and the Marquis, realising he was in the attics of what had once been a *Palazzo*, had to bow his head to enter.

He then saw that he was in a large attic which had been chosen by a painter because it had a sky-light.

Then he had eyes only for the low bed at the far end of it, on which lay a man.

Lucia had run towards him with a little cry, and now as she knelt down beside her father, the Marquis heard her say:

"Papa! Papa! Wake up! I have brought the Marquis of Wynchcombe to see you!"

For a moment there was no response, and the Marquis wondered if in fact Lucia's father was already dead.

Then as he reached the bedside he saw lying on it a man who must once have been extremely handsome, but who was now emaciated by either illness or starvation to little more than a skeleton of what he should have been.

Nevertheless, the broad forehead, the greying hair that swept back from it, and the fair skin proclaimed him to be an Englishman and a gentleman.

Very slowly, as the Marquis and Lucia waited, Bernard Beaumont opened his eyes.

They were sunk deep in his face, and the lines beneath them were the result of pain and privation.

But there was a faint smile on his pale lips as he managed to say in a low voice:

"This is—extremely—gracious of—Your Lordship."

"I am sorry to see you so ill," the Marquis said, "but your daughter tells me you have some paintings to sell."

"I—hope there are—some—left."

Then, as if the effort had been too much for him, Bernard Beaumont closed his eyes, and Lucia rose from her knees.

"He is very weak," she said in a low voice to the Marquis, "but I am glad that he recognised you."

She moved away from the bedside, and the Marquis now looked round the attic.

It contained little except for a painter's easel, a deal table in the centre of the room, and two chairs which had been roughly repaired with string.

There was what looked like a makeshift screen in one

corner of the room, which the Marquis was sure hid a couch or a bed on which Lucia slept.

Moving to the wall near the screen, Lucia discovered some canvasses that were stacked there.

As if she sensed that the Marquis was questioning their position, she explained:

"I was afraid they might fade in the sunlight, which can be very hot and strong at midday."

She carried one of the larger canvasses towards the Marquis as she spoke, and when she reached him she turned it round and lifted it up onto the easel, which was empty.

The Marquis looked at it, hoping he was not about to see the usual amateurish impression of Venice gaudily coloured and indifferently drawn.

On the other hand, it might be worse still and be merely a poor copy of one of the great paintings by Canaletto, Guardi, or Piazzetta, which had been copied a thousand times and never very successfully.

Instead, he found himself staring at something so unusual and so original that for the moment he found it hard to believe what he was seeing.

Without speaking, Lucia brought another painting from the pile against the wall to set it against the bottom of the easel, then two others to put on the chairs, and the last two against the legs of the table.

The Marquis did not speak.

He merely looked from the first painting to the next, then to the others she had brought.

Although they were very different from any paintings he had ever seen before, he knew, because he was a connoisseur and experienced in recognising what was right or wrong in an artist's work, that what he was seeing was revolutionary.

They were so different from the traditional style of the Venetian artists that he could understand that such paintings in Venice, more than anywhere else, would be unsaleable.

Slowly, as his eyes went from one to the other, he realised that what Beaumont had depicted was what he felt rather than what he saw.

He had managed, perhaps better than even Turner had done, to depict the translucency of the light which was characteristic of Venice, and at the same time to give an impression of life which other artists had attempted but failed.

For the moment, because the paintings were so unusual, he almost doubted his own ability to criticise them.

Then as he moved slowly so as to stand in front of each painting in turn, he knew that Beaumont was a genius.

Yet, the Marquis knew that because he was so far in advance of his time, it would be difficult if not impossible to recognise him, even for those who considered themselves authorities in appreciation of art.

The Marquis thought it was only because he himself was in some way attuned to the paintings and to what Beaumont was trying to say that he could realise how remarkable the paintings were.

It was in fact his instinct which told him that one day they would be acclaimed.

But his mind, logical and factual, was aware that Beaumont would for the present be either laughed at, scorned, or, worse still, ignored.

The Marquis was concentrating so intently on what he was seeing, and recognising the subtlety and the artistry of Beaumont's work, that he had forgotten for the moment that Lucia was there.

Just as he thought the paintings spoke to him and aroused a strange response within himself, so he felt that she did the same.

Without even looking at her he could feel her tenseness and that she was willing him with her whole being to approve what he was seeing.

He thought too that she was praying, and once again,

although she was very still, her fingers were locked together and the knuckles were white.

Then the Marquis looked at her face and saw her eyes, grey and flecked with gold in the sunlight, beseeching him without words to understand.

And he knew without being told that she was not at this moment asking for money.

She was wanting him, as an acknowledged collector and lover of art, to understand what her father had attempted to portray on canvass.

The Marquis looked down at her. Then he asked:

"Are these all your father's paintings?"

She looked away and he saw a faint flush stain the whiteness of her skin.

"There were... others."

"And what happened to them? Have you sold them?"

Again she hesitated before she said:

"A Dealer took one... but he did not expect to be... able to sell it. Two others I gave in... exchange for food, one to a butcher, the other to a small Café, who let me have their... stale bread at the... end of the day."

The Marquis did not speak, and she said:

"Do you... do you... like them?"

It was a simple question, and he knew that she awaited his answer almost as if she expected a blow.

"I think what you are asking me," the Marquis replied quietly, "is whether I will buy them."

"Would... you?"

He turned to look at her again, thinking that the anxiety in her eyes was so poignant, so intense, that it was almost too revealing to be anything but embarrassing.

Then he said quietly:

"I will buy these and any more you can get back from those who have them!"

For a moment it seemed as if Lucia did not understand what he was saying.

Then the pain in her eyes changed to a light that seemed to be part of the paintings themselves.

It was joined with the sunshine to seem dazzling and to dance and glitter as it did on water over the shabby poverty of the attic.

"You will . . . buy . . . them!"

She repeated the words as if to reassure herself.

"Your father is undoubtedly a genius," the Marquis said, "but I doubt if people will realise it for many years. He is too far in advance of his time."

Lucia drew in her breath and said in a voice that was barely audible:

"How . . . can you . . . understand? How can . . . you say anything so . . . wonderful?"

The Marquis saw the tears fill her eyes, making them seem larger and more luminous than they were already.

Then she turned with the swiftness of a bird in flight, and ran to the bed to throw herself down on her knees beside her father.

"Papa!" she said. "Listen . . . Papa, the Marquis will . . . buy your . . . paintings! He appreciates them . . . and says you . . . are a . . . genius!"

Very slowly Bernard Beaumont opened his eyes.

"You have—sold the—paintings?" he asked in a whisper.

"All of them, Papa! All we have . . . here!"

"You are—a clever—girl—Lucia," her father said, and shut his eyes again.

The Marquis had returned to the contemplation of the paintings.

It seemed extraordinary, he thought, that no-one had ever before thought of using that particular technique in depicting Venice.

And yet, now that he saw it, it seemed almost as if it were the only way to capture on canvass anything so beautiful, so elusive, and so dream-like.

Beaumont had made the water in the canals seem alive as others had failed to do.

There was life too rather than merely the perfection of architecture in the Palaces he had painted with the sun warming their ancient stones and making even the darkness of their door and windows seem to move.

Everything Bernard Beaumont had touched, the Marquis thought, appeared not only to glow but to breathe, and his paintings in some strange way made one not only remember only the past but think of the future.

He was aware that Lucia was standing beside him, and he said:

"First we must get your father well, then we must bring him back to England. I want him to paint my house in the country."

He saw the excitement in her expression and knew that for the moment she could not find words in which to answer him.

Then he said:

"But more important than anything else, you both need food. If I give you the money now, is there anybody who can go out and buy some for you?"

"I will go," Lucia said quickly.

"Alone?"

His voice told her what he was asking far more than his actual word.

She glanced out the window, as if the sunlight told her the time.

"Usually," she said, "while Papa is ill . . . I go very . . . early in the . . . morning. That was . . . how I saw . . . you."

The Marquis understood only too well that later in the day a woman as young and attractive as Lucia walking about alone would be followed and insulted by men.

He appreciated that it had been intelligent of her to go so early, when, as he had found, there was practically nobody about.

"Stay here," he said, and it was an order. "I will send you everything you require for today. Tomorrow, if he is well enough, I think you should move your father into better and more congenial surroundings."

He saw an expression of fear in her grey eyes and knew that she was afraid to go searching for a different place in which to live, in case what she wanted would be misunderstood because she was enquiring as a woman alone.

He acknowledged to himself that he made a mistake and said quickly:

"Leave everything to me. I will make all the arrangements for you. In the meantime, here is some money in case you need it, and what I will pay for the paintings would be best placed in a Bank."

As he spoke he drew from his pocket what money he had with him, and put it on the table.

It was not much, but at the same time he knew it would seem a lot to Lucia.

He saw that she was looking at it as if she did not believe it was real but like Fairy Gold would disappear.

"As soon as I return to my *Palazzo*," he said, "I will send you food and somebody to collect the paintings, and I will also instruct a Physician to call to see your father."

Lucia was silent for a moment. Then she said:

"The... Doctors in Venice are not... very good. I think... if they had been more experienced they would have... saved Mama from... dying. I am... sure that what Papa needs is food... and hope... and if you give him those... he will... live."

The Marquis smiled.

"Perhaps you are right. We will forget about the Doctor unless you ask me to obtain one for you. In the meantime, take care of yourself, and do not go walking about the streets alone."

"I will... stay with... Papa," Lucia replied, "and thank God for... you and... your kindness. I have no other way of... telling you how... grateful I... am."

The Marquis smiled at her, thinking that the gratitude in her voice was very moving and that the happiness he had given her made her eyes shine in a way he had never seen before in any other woman.

Almost as if he assured himself that she was real, he looked again at the paintings and saw that there was the same light in them.

A light so brilliantly expressed that it was almost as if the paints themselves had a magic quality in them, rather than the painter.

He opened the door and, bending his head carefully, went out onto the landing.

It was then, as he saw the dirt and dilapidation of what had once been a fine staircase, that he thought how incongruous it was that hidden here in the attics of a house that belonged to the past was a painter whose work undoubtedly belonged to the future.

He knew that Lucia was watching him as he went slowly down the stone steps, avoiding their broken edges and treading a little gingerly where they were cracked.

Only when he had reached the bottom floor and the door which was open into the *callete* outside did he look up.

He could see her face almost as if she were poised above him in the sky.

It struck him that she might easily be an angel or a goddess on one of the magnificently painted ceilings in the Doge's Palace.

Then as she made a movement with her hand in farewell, he realised that she was human, and yet as insubstantial and translucent as her father's paintings.

*　　*　　*

Travelling back over the Grand Canal in a gondola to his *Palazzo*, the Marquis felt as if what had just happened had been part of a dream or his imagination.

How could he have guessed when he had left Francesca sleeping in his bed that he would have such a strange adventure that in retrospect seemed incredible?

Incredible that in Venice, a City filled with artists of every sort and description and of every nationality, he should find an Englishman who could paint in such a strange and original manner that he was already doubting his own judgement of him.

"It is fantastic!" he assured himself. "At the same time, the man is a great artist, although I think there are only a few people who will feel as I do about him."

He was sure that the six paintings he had bought would confound a great number of those to whom he would show them, and doubtless they would prove controversial for a long time until he was acknowledged to be right in what he thought about them.

It was not difficult to be aware that fashion in art changed all the time.

At the beginning of the century, the Prince of Wales had been laughed at and thought a fool because he had bought Dutch paintings that had been out of favour for years.

And yet now already the Museums and Galleries were competing to add Dutch artists to their collections, and the King had crowed triumphantly over those who had criticised him.

"I will come into the same category," the Marquis told himself.

At the same time, he had a feeling that it would be years before Beaumont's particular style was acknowledged and then imitated.

'I shall then be able to laugh at those who undoubtedly will now think I have wasted my money,' the Marquis thought with satisfaction.

As the gondola he had hired came to rest outside his *Palazzo*, one of his servants hurried forward to help him out of it.

He stepped out with an alacrity that was unusual, feeling that he had a great deal to do.

He hurried up the long flight of stairs which took him to the main floor, where the State-Rooms were situated, including his own bedroom.

He imagined that Francesca would by this time have

returned to her own room, but he was taking no chances.

He went directly to the Dining-Room, where he knew breakfast would be waiting for him.

Before he seated himself at the table he sent a servant hurrying for Mr. Johnson, his secretary, and when a few minutes later he arrived, he gave him his instructions.

"You quite understand," the Marquis finished, "I want the food taken there with all speed. There is no time for the Chef to cook a great deal. He can do that later. Just tell him to heat the soup and put it in a hay-hamper. When that has been done, I will see him and give him further orders for later in the day."

"Very good, My Lord."

"Send Augustino with the food, and tell him he is to buy anything Miss Beaumont requires," the Marquis continued. "Then see if you can find them lodgings with a Studio in a better part of the City."

He knew his secretary looked at him in astonishment, but he was too well trained to ask questions, and the Marquis said:

"As Mr. Beaumont is ill, they will require a servant to tend him, so for the time being provide somebody from here—a man you can trust, and who will understand what is expected of him."

"Very good, My Lord."

The Marquis's secretary thought he had had many strange instructions during the years he had served a very exacting master, but this was certainly unusual.

"When the paintings arrive," the Marquis went on, as if he was following his own train of thought, "I want them hung for the time being in the Library."

"It will mean removing the paintings that are already there, My Lord."

"I am aware of that," the Marquis answered sharply. "Have them put somewhere carefully where they will not be damaged. I want to see the paintings I have bought on the wall, for that, I am sure, is the best place for them."

Mr. Johnson wrote down what he had been told, then

as he thought there were no more orders, he turned towards the door, but as an afterthought the Marquis said:

"Tell Augustino to inform Miss Beaumont that I shall be visiting her this afternoon, and ask him also to obtain from her the addresses where her father's other paintings were left or sold, and to buy them back."

"What price should he give for them, My Lord?"

"Whatever is asked. Do not prevaricate, but obtain them at any cost."

Again Mr. Johnson was surprised.

All the time he had been with the Marquis he had been aware that although he was extremely generous when it suited him, he very much disliked anybody taking advantage of him.

Picture-Dealers, tradesmen, wine-merchants, or anybody else who attempted to put up their prices because they knew he could afford it were swiftly disillusioned.

The Marquis paid what was right and just, and no more, and this was the first time, Mr. Johnson thought, that he had ever known him to give *carte blanche* for something he required.

There were obviously no more orders for the moment, and as the Marquis continued his breakfast Mr. Johnson left him alone.

By the time the Marquis left the Dining-Room it was far later in the morning than was usual.

He was therefore not surprised when as he went towards the room in which the paintings were to be hung, he heard the patter of two dainty feet following him.

He turned round to wait for Francesca.

She was fully dressed and looking exquisite, with her dark hair, which he knew had already received the attention of a hairdresser, hidden under a fashionable bonnet ornamented with emerald-green ostrich feathers.

There were emeralds in her small ears, and the Marquis remembered that he had promised her a necklace to match them.

However, he was sure that she would already have

arranged for a Jeweller to call on him later in the day.

Her dark eyes were gleaming under their mascarraed eye-lashes, and her red lips, which seemed always to be ready for kisses, were smiling at him provocatively.

"How could you let me wake to find you gone?" she asked in a manner that was both a reproach and a compliment.

"You were sleeping very soundly," the Marquis answered.

"I missed you," Francesca said, "but I cannot tell you how much at this moment, because I have a rehearsal. Tonight, because you have made me so happy, I will sing better than I have ever sung before."

"And I must of course say that is impossible," the Marquis replied a little mockingly.

Francesca laid her hand for a moment against his cheek.

"When I tell you I will sing for you," she said, "it is a present, and there will be another present for you later in the evening."

There was no doubt what she was insinuating, and the Marquis's eyes were slightly cynical as he raised her hand to his lips.

He was too well versed in the wiles of women not to realise that if they gave, they also expected to receive, and if the emerald necklace was in his mind, it was also very much in Francesca's.

"Until tonight," she said very softly.

She turned away, supremely confident that he would watch her walk down the long Gallery which ran down the centre of the *Palazzo* until she reached the stairs at the end of it.

He watched her, as was expected of him.

Then the swing of her fashionable and very expensive gown made him think unexpectedly that when Lucia had moved beside him in her unfashionable and threadbare clothes, her feet had hardly seemed to touch the ground.

And as they had climbed the long staircase to the

attics she had seemed to float upwards as if there were wings on her feet.

One reason was that she had been so thrilled and excited that he had consented to come with her.

But another was that she was so light through not having enough to eat that he thought poetically that she might stand on a rose-petal and not bruise it.

Then as Francesca disappeared from sight, the Marquis sent for his Chef and began to consider what was best to build up the strength of a man who was, he was convinced, dying from starvation.

"What could have made him get to such a state?" he wondered.

He felt unusually curious about Beaumont and how he had come to paint in such an unusual manner.

The Marquis found himself thinking of the artist and his daughter throughout the morning.

When just before luncheon he learnt that Augustino had returned with the paintings, he took the unusual step of going down himself to the entrance to see them being lifted from the gondola.

When they had been carried upstairs in the linen wrapping which Mr. Johnson had prudently provided, the Marquis, as they began to be unwrapped, had a sudden fear that he had been mistaken.

Supposing the light in the attic, or Lucia herself, had beguiled him into making a false judgement and seeing the paintings in a different perspective from what was the truth?

Perhaps after all they were just rubbish, the daubs of a man who could not portray adequately the architecture of Venice and therefore had resorted to painting light, rather than what was tangible.

Then as Mr. Johnson lifted the first painting from its cover, the Marquis knew that his instinct had not failed him.

The paintings were fantastic!

There was no other word for them, and while he still

was aware that few people would agree with him, he had by a stroke of unexpected luck discovered a new star in the world of art.

It was only when he had decided exactly where each painting should hang, and which of those that belonged to the owner of the *Palazzo* should be banished from their accustomed place, that Mr. Johnson reminded the Marquis that he had a luncheon engagement.

"The Count is expecting Your Lordship," he said, "and will undoubtedly be very disappointed if you fail to arrive."

"I had forgotten," the Marquis said.

He looked at the clock and said with a sigh:

"I suppose I had better go now. Have the paintings hung exactly where I have shown you, Johnson, and when I return I will let you know what I intend to pay for them and where the money should be deposited."

He did not wait for Johnson's reply, but went to his bedroom to change his coat for one which was smarter and had been cut by Weston, the tailor, who enjoyed the King's patronage.

"Yer Lordship dressed this mornin' without my assistance," his valet said reproachfully.

Because he had been with him for many years, Evans was, the Marquis knew, extremely jealous if he was overlooked or found that his master could manage without him.

"I was in a hurry to go out in the fresh air," he replied.

"Wot Yer Lordship's missin' is yer rides," Evans said in the tone of a Nanny reproving an obstreperous child. "I thinks Yer Lordship wouldn't be 'appy in a place without 'orses."

"You are right," the Marquis replied.

"If Yer Lordship asks me, the sooner we gets back in England, the better!" Evans said. "Yer Lordship wouldn't want to miss the races when there's at least three likely winners in Yer Lordship's stables."

The Marquis guessed that Evans was tempting him for reasons of his own.

At the same time, he had to admit that there was some truth in the valet's statement that he missed his rides and the large amount of exercise he habitually took when in England.

Evans did not say any more, but the Marquis had the feeling that he was pleading with him, and he thought irritably that this was a day when people did nothing else.

First Lucia, then Francesca, and now Evans.

'It is a pity they cannot leave me alone,' he thought to himself.

But he was honest enough to realise that if they did, it would be even more irritating.

To make his valet happy, he said aloud:

"Perhaps you are right, Evans, and as I have no wish to grow fat and lazy, the sooner we return home, the better!"

"That's good news, M'Lord, very good news!" Evans remarked. "I was thinkin' to meself, a place like this ain't natural, not with streets made of water an' not a 'orse or a dog to be seen."

He paused, then added as if he was speaking to himself:

"Only women, all flashing eyes and 'come hither' looks, for decent men to cope with."

The Marquis wanted to laugh, knowing that Evans was referring to Francesca, whom he had disliked from the very first moment she had arrived at the *Palazzo*.

Because it was inevitable that there should be an affinity between a master and his valet, to whom traditionally the master was no hero, the Marquis was aware that Evans had very strong likes and dislikes about the women in his life.

There was one "Incomparable" whom he had taken under his protection and set up in a house in Chelsea, and Evans had such abhorrence of her that the Marquis could feel hatred exuding from him when he was dressing to visit her.

She had not lasted long, and the Marquis had often thought with a mocking smile that when she had come to bore him, which was inevitable, Evans had hastened the process with his own type of witchcraft.

"Yer Lordship should be careful of these 'ere Venetians," Evans was saying now.

"In what way?" the Marquis enquired.

He had changed his cravat and was tying the one Evans had given him in an even more intricate and elaborate style than he had used first thing in the morning.

"I-talians, from all I 'ears, are bad enough wi' their vendettas and crimes o' passion," Evans answered, "but the Venetians, M'Lord, be subtle. Poison's more to their taste."

"I doubt it!" the Marquis replied loftily. "And it is always a mistake to listen to gossip."

"I'm just warnin' Yer Lordship."

"That is what I suspected," the Marquis replied, "but I assure you, Evans, there is no need for it."

As he spoke he walked from his dressing-room, knowing that Evans would be feeling discomfitted.

At the same time, he found it rather touching that the man should be so protective and think that he could not look after himself.

He stepped into the gondola, ready to be carried only a short distance along the canal to one of the most famous *Palazzos* which was still in possession of the family for whom it was originally built.

As he did so, he found himself thinking that after what would undoubtedly be a long-drawn-out meal, he would visit Lucia again and see if she had enjoyed the food he had sent her.

* * *

Lucia, at the time the Marquis was thinking of her, was actually feeding her father the soup which the Chef had sent in the hay-basket.

It was still hot when it arrived, and after she had given her father only a quarter of it she wrapped it up again to keep it warm.

She was wise enough to know that when anybody had been without food for a long time, it was a mistake to eat too much too quickly.

She had looked at the enormous hamper that the Italian servant had brought up the stairs and into the attic, and strangely enough had found that she was not hungry.

It was only when he had left her to try to trace the paintings of which she had disposed, as the Marquis had ordered him to do, that she made an effort to eat.

She nibbled tentatively a little of the cold salmon mousse which the Chef had arranged in one dish, and found it so delicious that she managed to dispose of quite a sizeable amount of it.

There was a light claret for her father, and this too she had fed him spoonful by spoonful, knowing that once again it would be a mistake to drink too much alcohol.

Now that he had had several more spoonfuls of the soup, she persuaded him to try a little of the salmon. After a while he seemed to enjoy a mouthful of chicken resting on a pasta so light that she felt it might float away.

"No—more," her father managed to say.

As he lay back against the pillows, Lucia felt there was a little more colour in his face, and his lips were not so bloodless as they had been earlier in the day.

"With food like this, Papa," she said, "you will soon be up and able to paint another picture for the Marquis, which is what he wants."

Her father did not answer, and she looked at him apprehensively, and because he was so still, she felt that he was drifting away from her and there was nothing she could do to stop him.

Then she told herself that she was worrying needlessly.

The Marquis had come to their assistance like an Archangel of deliverance, and now everything would be different.

39

'Perhaps we could even stay here,' Lucia thought, 'because Papa finds it easier to paint here than in England.'

Then with a little shiver she knew she would never feel safe unless she was with him.

Ever since her father had fallen ill and she had been obliged to go out by herself, she had realized the dangers that lurked in every doorway, on every bridge, and in every *callete*.

Men like menacing animals seemed to spring at her from every shadow.

While she had never noticed them before when she was with her father, now she was acutely aware of them, and her whole body shrank and shivered every time one of them came anywhere near her.

Once, when a man had pursued her, it was only because she could run faster than he that she had been able to escape.

She had dropped the parcels of food she had been carrying, the purchase of which had delayed her longer than she had intended so that it was later in the morning than usual.

With flying feet she had swept over the bridge of the canal nearest to their lodgings, and slipped in through the open door and up the stairs before her pursuer realised exactly where she had gone.

Only when she reached the attic door did she listen to hear if he was behind her, and when there was only silence, she felt that she must faint from sheer relief.

She stood there shivering and feeling as if the walls were swimming round her.

Then she told herself that she must not distress or upset her father by letting him know what had happened.

It was nearly five minutes before she had composed herself enough to breathe naturally, walk into their room, and make some plausible excuse as to why she had not brought back the food which she had gone out to buy.

As she could not walk about at a later hour, it also

prevented her from selling her father's paintings, or begging, as once or twice she had been obliged to do in order to pay their rent.

Now that she saw the money lying on the table where the Marquis had left it, she could hardly believe it possible that she could now pay what was owed.

There would also be enough left over to keep them in comfort for at least two more weeks.

Then she remembered that the Marquis would pay them for the paintings, and she knew that however much her father wanted to stay, they must return to England.

"I will not upset him, but I must explain that I cannot walk about alone," Lucia told herself.

She was aware that to her father she was still a child, and that because she had been very careful not to worry him, he had no idea that as a woman she was not safe in the streets of Venice.

Sometimes when she was frightened of leaving him to go out, she would look at herself in the cracked mirror which stood in a corner of the room in which she slept and wonder how she could make herself look old and ugly.

She had a feeling it was not only her face she would have to alter, but her figure, the way she walked, and of course the fairness of her skin, which was so different from that of the Venetian women.

With a sudden determination which had not been there before, she said now:

"We will go home and back to the village in the country where we lived for so long, and where nobody took any notice of us."

Thinking of it now with its small black-and-white thatched cottages, green fields, and trees which would be just coming into bud after the winter, it seemed to Lucia far more beautiful than Venice could ever be.

Then, thinking of the eulogies which her father and many other people had uttered about the City, she laughed at herself.

Then with irrefutable logic she thought:

'It is not what one's eyes see which matters. It is where one's heart is.'

It was that, she knew, which had made her mother supremely happy in Venice, because her heart was with her husband there.

To him, Venice was all he had dreamt of and all he had ever wanted to paint.

But Lucia thought passionately that she would give up the San Marco, the *Palazzos*, the Grand Canal, and the glory of the sky and sea for the village green at Little Morden.

To her, the duck-pond and their little cottage with primroses blooming in the garden were far lovelier than the Doge's Palace.

Then she told herself that she had been very wrong and untrusting not to believe that God, her mother, and her Guardian Angel had been looking after her.

They had sent her to the *Piazza* this morning at exactly the right time to see the Marquis sitting alone at the table outside Florian's Café.

She had known then, as if a voice from Heaven told her so, that this was her chance to speak to him.

She remembered very clearly the frist time she had ever seen him. It was at a Steeple-Chase arranged by the Duke of Madresfield, on whose Estate they lived in the village of Little Morden.

Because her mother had thought it would amuse her, she had suggested to her father, who was too immersed in his painting to be interested, that they should go to watch the Steeple-Chase.

He had looked up from his easel with a frown.

"Is that wise, my darling?" he had enquired.

"We need not go near the stand where the Duke and his friends will watch the race," her mother replied. "We can see the riders at the end of the course near the Folly."

Her father nodded as if he knew what she meant.

"We shall have a perfect view from there," his wife

continued, "and I know Lucia will enjoy seeing the men ride with an expertise that is something I used to enjoy watching when I was her age."

There was just a note of wistfulness in her mother's voice which Lucia had noticed was always there when she spoke of fine horses.

Although her mother and her father rode and she had a pony of her own, she knew that her mother did not feel they had the sort of horseflesh that she would wish to have for their small stable.

Although she never complained, there were times when she spoke of how she had ridden as a girl, and it brought a sparkle to her eyes and a lilt to her voice that was very revealing.

They had gone to the Steeple-Chase, and as the riders came thundering towards them to take the high fence that was directly below where they were sitting, Lucia had been aware that there was one man who was outstanding.

It was not only because he was in front of the rest of the field, but also because he appeared to ride better than anybody else and seemed to be part of the huge black stallion on which he was mounted.

He took the fence with a foot to spare.

Then as his horse landed faultlessly, he looked back over his shoulder to see how those following him had fared.

As he did so, there was a smile of triumph and satisfaction on his lips which told Lucia he would win the race with ease.

As he rode on, her eyes followed him, and as he took another fence a little way in the distance, her mother said:

"That was the Marquis of Wynchcombe. I saw in the newspaper that he was awarded a medal for gallantry at the Battle of Waterloo."

"He is a very good rider, Mama."

"It runs in his family," her mother had answered almost beneath her breath.

Then as the other riders passed them her father said:

"Let us go home. I want to finish my painting, and it depresses me, my darling, to know you are regretting that you cannot take the fences in the same style and ride the same sort of horses."

"That is where you are wrong," her mother had replied quickly. "You know I have no regrets about anything."

Despite the fact that there were a few other spectators present like themselves, her mother had bent forward and kissed her husband on the cheek.

Instantly his eyes lit up, dispelling an expression of anxiety as he asked:

"Do you mean that? Do you really mean it?"

"How can you ask such an absurd question?" Lucia's mother had replied. "Let us go back to what to me is the happiest and most perfect place in the whole world, and which I would not change for a thousand Palaces or ten thousand horses."

Her voice rang with a sincerity which was unmistakable, and Lucia watched her father put out his hands to pull her mother to her feet.

Then, linking his arm in hers, they had walked away over the rough grass, laughing together and saying things that only they could hear.

Lucia followed them.

But she was thinking of the Marquis, thinking of the way he had jumped the fence and the smile of triumph there had been on his lips.

She was only fifteen, but she had the feeling then that she had just seen an outstanding person.

She was sure that the Marquis was a man who would always win exactly what he wanted in life, whatever opposition there might be against him.

Chapter Three

The Marquis found himself growing impatient as the luncheon with its inevitable dishes of pasta seemed to be more drawn out than usual.

His host belonged to one of the oldest Venetian families, and the rest of the guests were all aristocrats to their fingertips, and very conscious of it.

They talked politics, and once again the iniquities of the Austrians were enumerated, criticised, and mouthed over until the Marquis found himself beginning to yawn.

The *Palazzo* in which the party took place was redolent with history but was also, the Marquis noticed, badly in need of restoration.

It was sad that so many Palaces, houses, Churches, and monuments were neglected in Venice. At the same time, he could not help feeling that it was entirely the fault of the Venetians themselves.

If they had spent less time in frivolous enjoyment, they might easily have kept their Republic independent and continued to be prosperous and important, as they once had been.

However, it was no use regretting the past, the Marquis thought, and he tried to encourage them to take a more optimistic view of the future.

But when he left the party he felt that they had neither the spirit nor the determination to amend their lot.

Instead, they just grumbled against their Austrian overlords and made the lives of those who had to serve the Emperor in Venice as uncomfortable as possible.

As his gondola sped away from the *Palazzo* into the sunshine, he found himself looking forward to seeing Lucia again and talking, if it was possible, to Bernard Beaumont.

The Grand Canal glittering in the sunshine reminded the Marquis of Turner's painting of it, and yet he thought that the one painted by Beaumont which he now owned was even more impressive.

Then he told himself that it was absurd to be so obsessed by an unknown artist, and doubtless when the paintings were hung on the walls of the *Palazzo* he would find a hundred flaws and even be convinced that the artist's whole conception of light was wrong.

He was certain that that was what other art-lovers would tell him!

At the same time, his instinct still told him very clearly that whatever they might say, they would be wrong, while he was right.

As the gondola moved on, making for the small canal which would bring him as near as possible to the house where Beaumont occupied the attic, the Marquis was questioning in his mind whether all great artists painted what they felt emotionally rather than exactly what they saw with their eyes.

The question had not occurred to him until now, but he knew that Beaumont's interpretation of Venice appealed to him in a way which he had to admit aroused a personal involvement and was a subtle appeal to his sensitivity.

This was something he had seldom felt before when looking at a painting.

At the same time, some cynical, practical part of his mind wanted to argue that such an attitude was just an illusion, and that when he saw Lucia again he would perhaps feel very differently about her.

The gondola drew up beside a bridge, and as the

Marquis stepped out he recognised a narrow *callete* running between high bridges and knew at the end of it was the turning which would lead him to the house where Lucia had taken him this morning.

He told the gondola to wait, and walked through the old quarter thinking that the washing hanging from some of the windows and the ragged children playing down near the canal were all evidence of extreme poverty.

However, there were balconies of delicate marble flanked by carved lions which had been erected in more prosperous times.

There were also ancient stone shields on the walls which the Marquis felt could tell a story of valour and victories which were now lost in the Venetians' glorious past.

He walked on until he came to the door of the high building where Lucia lived.

As he reached it the Marquis had a sudden impulse not to go in but to return to his own *Palazzo*.

He had a strange feeling that if he became any more involved with Beaumont, his daughter, and his paintings, it might have far-reaching consequences in his personal life.

He had no idea why he should feel this way, and he thought it was both strange and unpleasant.

At the same time, the feeling was there, and it was almost as if he was being urged to go no farther, while on the other hand it was something he wished to do.

"It must be the wine I drank at luncheon," he told himself.

Then, with what was almost an effort, he started to climb the dilapidated and dirty staircase which twisted and turned up to the top floor.

When he reached it he stood for a moment as he had before looking out over the roofs of Venice.

He could see the great shining domes of the San Marco and the tall, square tower of the Campanile.

The Marquis remembered that its gilded angel,

glittering in the sun, had served once as a landmark for the fleets of galleys bringing the riches of the Orient to Europe.

They had sailed into Venice, their holds filled with silks, spices, slaves, jewels, manuscripts, antique carvings, and relics.

It was their trading which had made the Venetians so rich and prosperous, and it was their frivolity and stupidity which had lost them their near monopoly on bringing to Europe the goods every country was longing to buy.

Then as the sunshine seemed to envelop what he was seeing with a glitter of gold which could no longer be translated into money, the Marquis turned to the door beside him and knocked on it.

It was opened almost instantly by Lucia, who he thought looked different from how he remembered her.

It was not only that she was wearing a coloured gown instead of the black one in which he had first seen her and which he knew she had worn because she wished to attract as little attention as possible.

It was in fact the first time that he could see her hair uncovered, and it was different from what he had expected.

He had realised that she was fair, which came from her English blood, but her hair was in fact so pale that it was the colour of the sun in the very early morning.

Even so, in the afternoon light there were touches of gold in it, and the gold was also reflected in the grey of her eyes.

As she came through the door of the room out onto the landing where the Marquis was standing, she seemed even more insubstantial than she had when he had first seen her.

Her figure was so slight from privation that she seemed more like a child than a woman.

She looked up at him, her eyes very large in her heart-shaped face, and said in a low voice:

"Papa is sleeping. I thought... My Lord, if you... did come to see me... we could talk... elsewhere."

"Of course," the Marquis agreed. "Where do you suggest?"

She made a little gesture towards the stairs up which he had just climbed and said:

"There is a place at the back of the building which is quiet."

"Then let us go there," he agreed with a smile.

He started to descend the stairs up which he had just climbed.

As he did so, he noted that while he chose carefully where he should put his feet on the cracked and broken steps, Lucia moved down them surefootedly and gracefully.

When they reached the door onto the street, Lucia moved instead down another passage, which led to the back of the building.

Here there was a door which led them down a few steps and across a dilapidated, paved and walled garden that might once have been filled with flowers and statues.

At the end of it was another small canal.

There was a stone seat where doubtless in days gone by the owners of the house had waited for their guests, or perhaps young people had made assignations without their parents' knowledge.

Even now it was still a romantic spot, with the dark water of the canal reflecting like a mirror the tall houses sweeping up on both sides of it to a blue sky.

Lucia sat down on the stone seat, which was carved at either end with a Venetian lion, chipped and cracked but still recognisable, and as the Marquis seated himself beside her she said:

"I . . . do not know how to begin to . . . thank Your Lordship for the food you sent us. Papa looks a little better already . . . and now he has fallen into a sleep of contentment, which is . . . something he has not . . . done for a . . . long time."

"I hope you, too, have eaten," the Marquis replied. "I do not need to tell you that you are much too thin."

She laughed, and it revealed little lines at the sides of

her mouth which the Marquis knew were there solely because she was undernourished.

"I had forgotten such marvellous food existed," she said, "and Papa enjoyed the wine . . . although I would only let him have a . . . very little of . . . it."

"I have given orders to my Chef to cook you a great deal more food," the Marquis said. "It will be sent to you tonight, and I have told my secretary to find you better lodgings with a Studio where your father can work again as soon as he is well enough."

Lucia clasped her hands together and said in a voice that trembled:

"How can . . . you be so kind? At the same time . . . we must not . . . impose on you."

"You are not doing that," the Marquis answered, "and I have decided into which Bank I will pay the money for your father's paintings."

There was a little silence. Then Lucia said:

"I think . . . when he is well enough . . . it would be wisest for us to . . . return immediately to . . . England."

"Why do you think such urgency is important?" the Marquis enquired.

She did not answer, and after a moment he said:

"I asked you a question, and I think you have a reason for not answering it."

She gave him a little glance which told him without words that she was surprised at his being so perceptive, before she said reluctantly:

"You will think . . . it is a strange thing for me to say . . . and that I am just . . . imagining things . . . but I am absolutely convinced that we should return to England now . . . in case Papa . . . leaves me here . . . alone."

She spoke as if the Marquis compelled her to tell the truth, and after a moment he said:

"If that is what you feel, then I think you are right. I will instruct my Courier to find a ship sailing for England in which your father will be comfortable without incurring too much expense."

"If Your Lordship . . . would do that . . . it would be . . . very kind."

"I have already told you," the Marquis said, "that when you reach England I would like your father to paint my house in Buckinghamshire. I will give you my address so that you can get in touch with me as soon as he is well enough to undertake the commission."

Lucia gave a little sigh as she said:

"Your kindness is overwhelming, My Lord, and for Papa to know that he has something definite to do in England will make it easier for me to . . . persuade him to leave Venice."

"I feel almost as if I am committing a crime in taking him away from the views he has painted so beautifully and so differently from anybody else," the Marquis said. "At the same time, England can be beautiful too."

"Very, very beautiful!" Lucia agreed with a rapt little note in her voice.

"I can see you love your country," the Marquis remarked, "and yet in a way you do not look entirely English."

He made the remark casually because he was thinking that her fair hair and the grey of her eyes, fringed by lashes that were darker than might have been expected, gave her somehow a faintly "foreign" look.

She stiffened and glanced away from him so that all he could see was her profile, and he was almost sure that there was a faint touch of colour in her cheeks that had not been there before.

"Am I right?" he asked. "You are not English?"

"Of course I am English!" Lucia replied quickly. "How could I be anything else when I am Papa's daughter?"

She spoke so positively that the Marquis looked at her in surprise.

At the same time, he was almost sure that there was some mystery about her ancestry and that he had been right in thinking she was not wholly English, although why it should matter he had no idea.

51

Barbara Cartland

Then, as if she was afraid he would go on asking her questions, Lucia said:

"I am sure Your Lordship has many things to do this afternoon, and I must not take up your time."

She rose from the seat as she spoke, and the Marquis rose too, wondering if he could force her into an admission about herself, then decided it would be unkind, and anyway it was not important.

They walked back to the house, and as they did so Lucia said:

"If Papa improves and Your Lordship is kind enough to pay us the money for his paintings, I am sure we will be able to leave here in a week or ten days' time."

"It will of course depend on what ship is available," the Marquis answered.

"There are always ships in the harbour, and I am sure that at this time of the year, when the visitors are beginning to arrive in Venice, there will be ships returning to England in which there will be room for us."

She spoke almost as if she was determined that there would be accommodation available, and the Marquis thought with a faint smile that however much her father wished to remain in Venice, she would doubtless overrule any objections he might make.

As they reached the house he turned and looked back, and he thought that the contrast of the sunshine with the deep shadows cast by the high houses made a very attractive picture.

"If your father was with us, Lucia," he said, "I am sure he would want to paint this."

"He has already painted it several times."

"You have not shown me those paintings or told me of them," the Marquis commented.

"I am not keeping anything from you," she answered quickly. "It was just that when we grew poorer and poorer, Papa could not afford to buy any more canvasses, so when he had painted a picture, he erased it and started again."

The Marquis groaned.

"What a waste! What a terrible waste of his genius!"

"I thought that at the time, but there was nothing I could do about it," Lucia replied.

"How can you have become so poor?"

She hesitated, and he wondered if she would tell him the truth. Then she said:

"When Papa and Mama decided to come here two years ago, it was because Papa was certain that his paintings of Venice would be so... good and unusual that he would be acclaimed... and perhaps make a great deal of... money."

Lucia spoke hesitatingly, and the Marquis knew she was finding it hard to put into words exactly what had happened.

"Go on," he prompted as she paused. "I am very interested."

"Papa had made a little money painting conventional pictures, which he hated doing, for the local people where we were living."

Lucia glanced at the Marquis, then explained:

"They were not grand people who could pay a lot of money. There was the Mayor of the Market Town near our village, two or three fairly wealthy farmers who wanted portraits of themselves and their wives, and one old lady who wanted her garden immortalised on canvass."

The way Lucia spoke made the Marquis smile, and she said:

"Papa hated every one of them! He felt as though he was degrading himself in painting what was saleable rather than what he believed was the real image of what he saw."

"I can understand that," the Marquis said.

"Very few people would understand," Lucia answered. "When he had finished the old lady's garden, he said to Mama:

"'I must get away! I feel as if I am being constrained, chained to this place, and that it is imprisoning not me but my soul!'"

"Your mother understood?"

"Of course she understood," Lucia answered. "She and Papa loved each other so completely that if he had asked her to live on top of the Himalayas, or in a cave at the bottom of the sea, she would have agreed."

There was a little throb in Lucia's voice which told the Marquis that the love between her father and mother had been very real to her too.

As he waited for her to continue her story, he thought that he could almost read what she was saying in the expressions which flickered in her grey eyes.

"They gave up the little cottage in which we had lived ever since I can remember," Lucia continued. "In fact, I was born there. Papa sold the furniture and everything we possessed, except for what we were taking with us."

"Surely that was somewhat drastic?" the Marquis remarked.

"Papa said we were starting a new life and it was always a mistake to be cluttered and encumbered when one was setting out on a crusade."

"And did your mother mind?"

"Mama thought it was as exciting as I did, and we were so certain that Papa would succeed."

Her expression was very revealing as she said:

"Papa wanted to be rich and important not for himself but for us. There was so much he wanted to give us: horses, gowns, and the possibility of going to London occasionally to attend the Opera and of course to see the paintings in the Royal Academy and the Galleries, which we had read about in the newspapers."

She gave a deep sigh as if now she realized it had only been a dream.

"So you came to Venice," the Marquis remarked.

"At first it was all very thrilling and everything Papa had hoped."

Then as she remembered what had happened, the Marquis saw her eyes cloud over, and as she was silent he asked quietly:

"Why did things go wrong?"

"Everything was much more...expensive than we had anticipated...and our money dwindled quickly...while nobody was...interested in the pictures which...Papa painted."

It was what the Marquis had expected to hear, and he knew by the note in Lucia's voice how worrying it had been, as she said:

"Then, when Mama was beginning to think we should return to England, she became ill."

"What was wrong?"

"I think it was the water that upset her, and also the cold of the winter, which somehow we had not expected. She grew worse...and because we had no money...Papa painted some ordinary pictures of Venice, which he was able to sell...but for very small sums."

"By 'ordinary,'" the Marquis observed, "I presume you mean the sort of paintings that visitors expect to be able to buy of the most beautiful City in the world."

"Exactly," Lucia agreed. "And Papa hated doing them because he said they were 'daubs' and had no artistic feeling. But because he asked very little for them, they were displayed in a shop in the *Piazza* and sold almost as soon as he finished them."

The Marquis could understand how degrading it must have been for a painter like Beaumont to have to prostitute himself in such a manner.

"Then, after Mama...died...Papa was only happy when he was...concentrating on the type of pictures he enjoyed painting...and because I did not wish to worry him...I suppose it was my fault that...things got so...bad."

She gave a deep sigh before she said:

"Just when I was...determined to make Papa paint the pictures which would sell...he too became ill."

Now in Lucia's voice there was the fear which the Marquis had heard before, and he said quickly:

"I do not want you to go on with your story if it upsets you."

"It is best that you know the truth," she said, "and I blame myself. Papa had always been...hopeless about money when he was painting and could think of nothing else...I should have been more like Mama...and made him understand that we should return home as soon as she...died."

Looking at her standing beside him, seeming so small and frail, the Marquis thought that Beaumont ought to have looked after his daughter better.

How could he have expected anyone so young and insubstantial to be practical?

Then, as if once again she understood what he was thinking, Lucia said quickly:

"You must not blame Papa, because he was so supremely confident that his paintings were real art...and would be appreciated by those who understand."

There was a sob in her voice as she went on:

"He had no idea that we could come to the very...edge of...starvation and nobody...except Your Lordship would...appreciate his paintings."

She drew in her breath before she said very quietly:

"I...I was thinking last night that...God had sent you to us at the...last possible moment."

"I think you had something to do with it!" the Marquis replied drily.

"If I did...I can only say again how...grateful I am," Lucia answered.

She gave him a smile that was like the sunshine itself.

Then, as if she felt she might have bored him by what she had said, she added quickly:

"I must go back to Papa and see if he is awake."

"I will come with you," the Marquis said.

As she spoke Lucia turned to enter the house, but then she stopped to say:

"You are...quite certain that it is something you ...wish to do?"

"As I am sure you realise, I very seldom do anything I do not want to do. So the answer is 'yes'!"

Lucia gave a little laugh.

"I was sure that was the truth . . . in which case . . . despite being wonderfully kind . . . you must also be very . . . spoilt."

It was something no-one had ever dared to say to the Marquis before, and he looked at her in surprise as she said quickly:

"I . . . I am sorry if that was rude, but because you are so overwhelming, I feel you have the whole world at your feet! Therefore, it must be difficult to be like other men . . . who are always . . . grasping and . . . striving for something that is . . . out of reach."

They were at the bottom of the stairs by this time, and as Lucia put her hand on the bannister, the Marquis looked at her in surprise.

"I think that is a rather strange thing to say," he said, "and yet I understand what you are implying. At the same time, like everybody else, I have my ambitions and wish to 'catch a falling star.'"

He knew by the smile on Lucia's lips that she recognised the quotation from John Donne, and it rather surprised him.

"Once again I am being rude, and you must forgive me," she said. "It is just that you seem so omnipotent, so unlike ordinary men, and I cannot really believe you are human."

The Marquis laughed.

"I am not certain if that is a compliment or an insult."

"A compliment," she said quickly. "Not that Your Lordship needs it!"

The Marquis laughed again.

"I hope, Miss Beaumont, that in the future I shall not disillusion you, but I assure you that I am in fact very human."

His eyes twinkled as he continued:

"In order to convince you, I will say that had I not been really impressed by your father's paintings and been sure that he is a genius, I would not have shown you the kindness for which you are thanking me, and would have 'passed by on the other side.'"

"But because you did ... understand what Papa was trying to say," Lucia said in a low voice, "it makes you ... different from anybody else, and, as I have already said ... very wonderful!"

The Marquis thought he had had many compliments in his life, but this was certainly different from any he had received before.

He knew as they climbed the stairs that Lucia was not thinking of him as an attractive man, as every other woman he met had done.

To her he was a super-human being who had swept down from the sky at the last moment to save her and her father from destruction.

He was not certain how he knew exactly what she was feeling, and yet he was sure that it was the truth.

They walked to the top of the stairs in silence, and when Lucia opened the door of the attic and went in, the Marquis followed her.

The sunshine coming through the sky-light cast a golden circle on the bare boards of the floor, but beyond it, where Beaumont was sleeping, the room was in shadow.

Lucia walked quickly towards him, but as she reached the bed she saw that her father was still asleep, and said in a low voice:

"Papa! Wake up, Papa! His Lordship is here, and I know you want to thank him for his kindness."

"Let him sleep ..." the Marquis began to say.

Then he saw laid out on the table the food he had sent from the *Palazzo*, and thought that as Lucia was building up her father's strength, it would be a good idea for him to be fed again before he went back to sleep.

He was sure that she felt the same thing as she leant over her father and said:

"Wake up, Papa! You have slept for quite a long time."

Then the Marquis, watching her, saw her put out her

hand to touch her father's where it lay outside the sheet, and as she did so she stiffened.

Anticipating what she felt, he moved towards her.

Then, holding on to her father's hand, she said in a different tone of voice:

"Papa! Papa!"

There was no response, and she put her other hand on his forehead and must have found it as cold as his hand was.

She gave a little cry which was frantic.

Then as the Marquis reached her, she said in a voice that was almost incoherent:

"It . . . cannot be! . . . How could it? Oh . . . no . . . ! It is . . . not true!"

Her voice broke on the last word, and she turned almost like a child might have done towards the Marquis, as if he would convince her that she was mistaken.

He put out his arm to support her, and as he looked down at Bernard Beaumont, he was aware that he was dead.

There was a smile on his lips, he looked happy and relaxed, but there was no mistaking that he had died quietly in his sleep and there was no life left in his body.

Because it was the only thing he could say, the Marquis remarked very quietly:

"He did not suffer, and you must be grateful for that."

"I . . . I cannot . . . lose him . . . how can he leave me . . . ?" Lucia faltered.

Then, as if she could not believe it was true, she hid her face against the Marquis's shoulder and burst into tears.

There was nothing else he could do but hold her closely and feel her tremble convulsively against him, her whole body shaking with the misery and despair of losing the only person who mattered in her life.

As he held her in his arms, the Marquis knew that in the darkness of her sorrow she was not even aware that he was there or that she was crying against him.

She was just lost in an unhappiness and despondency that was so overwhelming that for a moment she could not think, but was as lost as if she were left alone on the moon or an uninhabited planet.

"H-how . . . can he . . . leave me?" she asked again.

The Marquis felt that it was a question she was asking of the God in whom she believed.

He felt her tears abating a little. Then he said very quietly:

"I think your father would rather have died than find himself helpless and unable to paint, and I am sure he was glad that his paintings had been sold to somebody who would appreciate them."

As if his words reached her, Lucia said:

"He was . . . glad! When we talked . . . about it last night . . . he said he would rather . . . you owned them than . . . any other man in . . . England."

The Marquis looked down at the face of the painter and said:

"I think when your father died he knew that one day not only I but a great number of other people would proclaim his work. That is why he is smiling."

Very slowly Lucia raised her head from his shoulder and, without moving away from the Marquis, looked at her father.

"He . . . he does look . . . happy," she said thoughtfully after a moment.

"Very happy," the Marquis agreed, "and that is why you must not cry for him, Lucia, but try to be brave, as he would want you to be."

"How can I be . . . brave when I am . . . all alone?"

The Marquis knew as she spoke that it was not really a question to which she expected an answer, and yet, almost before he thought of it, he found himself saying:

"I will take you back with me to England, where I am sure you have relatives or friends who will look after you."

As if she was aware of him for the first time, Lucia looked up at him to ask:

"Did you really . . . say that you . . . would take me . . . back to England?"

"Yes, I am returning myself, and you can come with me."

"I . . . I must not be . . . a nuisance . . . but I cannot stay here . . . alone."

Now there was a note of fear in her voice which told the Marquis that she was afraid, as she had been when she told him about the men in the *Piazza*.

He was aware of how much it had frightened her when they pursued her because she was so young and lovely.

He quickly made up his mind, and as usual when he made decisions he swept away any opposition there might be.

"Fetch your bonnet, or whatever you wear on your head," he said. "I am taking you back now to my *Palazzo*. I will arrange your father's Funeral. Just leave it to me."

He felt her tremble against him before she said:

"Thank you . . . I would not . . . know what to . . . do."

"I realize that," he answered, "so you must just leave everything in my hands."

She looked at him, and he saw her eyes were still wet with the tears that had also run down her cheeks. And yet, unlike most women who cried, she looked, he thought, even lovelier than she had before.

"H-how . . . can I allow you to be so . . . kind?" she asked.

"It is not a question of allowing," the Marquis replied, "it is what I intend to do. There is no point in your staying here alone and upsetting yourself. I will arrange everything."

She looked at him for a long moment as if she could hardly believe what he was saying to her.

Then she moved from the shelter of his arms and went down on her knees beside the bed.

She bent her head, and the Marquis knew that she

was praying for her father's soul and was sure that wherever he was, he was with her mother.

They were together and happy to know that their daughter was being looked after.

How he knew such a thing he had no idea.

He was only aware that it was almost as if Bernard Beaumont had actually said to him: "Look after Lucia," and it was something he had to do.

Yet, some cynical part of his mind was asking him if he realised what he was undertaking, and why he should concern himself with some beggar-girl he had met only that morning.

If he were sensible he would simply provide her with enough money to get her to England, and forget her.

Then as he looked down at Lucia's bowed head, the fairness of it was somehow strange against the darkness of the unpainted walls and the bare floor.

He thought that with her dead father beside her it was a situation in which he had never found himself before, and certainly it was something which he had never anticipated would happen.

But it had, and just as Beaumont's paintings had been a surprise and in fact a revelation, so he was surprised at himself and by his behaviour.

He knew that in committing himself to taking Lucia back to England, he was doing something that might have far-reaching repercussions.

"I am making a mistake," the Marquis's brain told him.

And yet when he looked at Lucia again, he knew he could not abandon her.

"It would be an unkind and certainly a most unsporting thing to do," he argued in his own defence.

Then his mind asked him if there was not a British Consulate in Venice which could cope adequately with the situation, especially if he gave the girl enough money for her passage home.

'That is what I ought to do,' the Marquis thought.

As he did so, Lucia raised her head, and he saw that she was no longer crying.

But as she looked at her father, then raised her eyes to the ceiling above, there was a light in them and an expression on her face which made the Marquis draw in his breath.

It was as if she were seeing a vision, and because in some strange way he was attuned to her, he could see it too.

For a moment she was not on earth, but in a spirit-world to which her prayers and her love of her father had carried her.

She was touched with the light of the Divine, which seemed to vibrate through her, giving her a radiance which the Marquis knew in some strange way was the same radiance which vibrated from her father's paintings.

It was life itself, the life which comes from God, and which pours through all living things to a greater or lesser degree according to their capabilities.

As he looked at Lucia, her face seemed transparent, and he felt that if she slowly vanished before his eyes, he would not be in the least surprised.

Then as if she left the spheres to which her prayers and her love had carried her, she came back to earth.

The radiance in her eyes vanished, to be replaced by the sorrow and misery of loss.

She looked once again at her father, then bent forward to kiss gently his cold cheek.

Slowly she rose to her feet, and as she did so she seemed suddenly to be aware that the Marquis was there, waiting for her.

Like a child who wishes to be comforted, she slipped her hand into his, and as she did so, with her eyes still on her father, she whispered:

"He . . . is with . . . God."

She spoke softly, almost beneath her breath, and as

the Marquis's fingers closed over hers, he replied in a voice which he did not recognise:

"Of course he is—and with your mother!"

* * *

The Marquis drew Lucia across the room towards the makeshift screen behind which, on his first visit, he had sensed that she slept and kept her clothes and her few belongings.

"Get what you want now," he said quietly. "I will send somebody to pack up the rest later."

She looked at him a little uncertainly, and again, because he had a perception which made him aware of what she was feeling, he knew she was finding it hard to come back to earth.

"Are you . . . sure that is . . . what I should . . . do?"

"Quite sure!" he said positively. "As you are well aware, there is nothing now to keep you here."

"Perhaps I should not . . . leave Papa."

"I think you know that he does not need you and would tell you to go with me."

As if he persuaded her, Lucia let go of his hand and walked behind the screen.

The Marquis looked round the attic, and as if he was seeing it for the first time he thought how incongruous it was that such a sordid, drab place should have held Lucia and the pictures that Beaumont had painted.

He thought that when they had both gone there would be nothing left behind but death, then was surprised at his own thoughts.

Lucia came from behind the screen, and he saw that she was wearing a light shawl over her gown, and a bonnet of plain straw trimmed with blue ribbons on her fair hair.

He thought it was somehow sensible of her not to insist on black the moment her father was dead.

He remembered women he had known in London who draped themselves in crêpe almost before their husbands were cold, in an effort to dramatise their mourning.

"I am . . . ready," Lucia said, "but . . . please . . . I must ask you once again . . . you are quite . . . sure you want me to . . . come with you?"

"I am not only sure," the Marquis replied, "but I intend to take you away with me."

As he spoke he took her hand again and drew her towards the door, and as they reached it, Lucia looked back at her father as if for the last time.

Then, as if she forced herself to act naturally and to control the tears which the Marquis was certain were not far from the surface, she walked beside him down the stairs.

When they were in his gondola and were sitting side by side on the soft seats, she said in a very small voice:

"When you . . . arrange Papa's . . . Funeral . . . will you please . . . deduct the money it will cost . . . from what you were . . . going to give . . . us for his . . . paintings?"

Because it was the first thing she had said since leaving the house, there was a faint smile on the Marquis's lips.

It was somehow what he had expected Lucia might say, and he was aware that she was trying not to force herself upon him or to be more of an encumbrance than she could help.

He thought of how almost every woman he had ever known had expected him, because he was so rich, to pay for everything that concerned them.

Now it flashed through his mind that Francesca would be waiting tonight to receive the emerald necklace he had promised her.

"I told you to leave everything in my hands," he said quietly, "and I am looking forward to your seeing your father's paintings hung in the right type of background for them when we arrive at my *Palazzo*."

He saw Lucia's eyes light up before she asked in a worried little voice:

"Will there be a . . . lot of people there? And will they not think it . . . strange that I should be . . . arriving with you?"

"There will be no-one there when we arrive," the Marquis assured her.

As he spoke he remembered that Francesca would be returning later in the evening, but he thought that was a bridge he could cross later.

He was aware that Lucia immediately relaxed a little upon learning that she need not be afraid of meeting a large number of strangers. Then she said:

"Will you tell me... please... what I am to... do, and exactly how I should . . . behave? Mama would have ...known...but I have never been in a big house...neither in England nor here . . . and I am aware that I am very... ignorant."

"Just be yourself," the Marquis answered, "and I promise I will tell you what to expect, so that you will not feel shy."

"Thank... you."

Her tone expressed very much more than the actual words.

They moved down the Grand Canal, and as they looked at the Rialto Bridge, the Marquis knew that she was seeing it as her father had painted it.

It was almost as if he could look through her eyes and see everything seeming to glow with life—the water, the *Palazzos*, the bridge ahead, and the gondolas.

Even the people themselves seemed to live and breathe and, in some way the Marquis could not understand, to reach out towards something higher and greater than themselves.

It could only, he thought, be expressed in the way Lucia had looked when she had prayed at her father's bedside.

He was wondering how he could possibly know—or rather feel—such a thing as Lucia was feeling, when he felt her slip her hand into his.

"Thank... you," she said again.

The two words, like the touch of her fingers, seemed to convey to him the vibrations of life.

Chapter Four

*T*he Funeral Service in the little Anglican Church of St. George was very quiet and moving.

There were no other mourners apart from Lucia and the Marquis, and her father's coffin was carried in state in an ornate Funeral Gondola with its canopy of black and silver.

The Marquis understood how everything had been done so quickly when Mr. Johnson told him that the owner of the house in which the Beaumonts had rented the attic wanted the dead man removed as swiftly as possible.

"The Italians think it unlucky to have a corpse lying for long, My Lord," Mr. Johnson had explained, "and I therefore agreed that by paying a great deal extra the Funeral could take place today. Fortunately, in this part of the world coffins are ready for just such emergencies."

The Marquis was not particularly interested in the details, but he knew that for Lucia's sake it would be best for her not to worry about her father's body being left unattended in the attic from which he had taken her.

Therefore, it was after luncheon the following day that they watched Bernard Beaumont's coffin carried down the dilapidated staircase and into the black gondola and then followed it down the Grand Canal to the Campo San Vio.

The Marquis appreciated that Lucia was very brave during the Service and the subsequent Funeral on the cemetery island of San Michele.

She had not cried, and only when the coffin was lowered into the ground did he realise that she was fighting her tears, and then he took her hand in his.

He felt her fingers tremble and knew she was exerting a control over herself and her behaviour, which he admired.

He had always disliked passionate expressions of grief and had endured enough dramatics from the King when he was young to last him, as he had said to Alastair, for the rest of his life.

As they had left the Church-yard, Lucia had thanked the Parson in a quiet, calm voice.

The Marquis thought there were few women, however well bred or aristocratic, who would have behaved with the same fortitude.

When they were moving away from the island back towards the City, he said quietly:

"Your father would have been proud of you."

"I . . . hope so," Lucia replied, "but I did not . . . feel it was Papa who was . . . buried in the ground . . . just his body."

She spoke almost as if to herself, and the Marquis said:

"Now you have to think about yourself and your future."

She did not reply but just looked ahead in the direction in which they were going, and he understood how terrifying it must be to be alone with only strangers in such circumstances.

However, he supposed that she must have relatives in England and thought that later he would talk to her about them and help her to decide with whom she should get in touch when she arrived back in her own country.

For the moment it would be best to speak of other things, and the obvious subject was Venice.

The sunshine shimmering over the lagoon made it look as if it were part of a fairy-tale and without reality.

Everywhere the Marquis looked he thought that this was the light which Beaumont should have immortalised on canvass, as Bellini, Carpaccio, Tiepolo, and Canaletto had tried to do before him.

There was no doubt that the light of Venice was different from that of any other place. It was a particularly clear light but never, the Marquis thought, as sharp as that in Greece.

In the evening it could have a rare apricot tinge. But whatever it was like at whatever time of day, the Marquis acknowledged that it had a mysterious enchantment.

"It is the mystery of poetry," he told himself, and thought the same words could apply to Lucia.

Following the train of his thoughts, he asked her:

"Have you ever tried to paint?"

Lucia turned her eyes towards him, and as if she came back from a long distance she replied after a moment:

"I have no . . . talent for it like . . . Papa."

"Then what are you good at?"

"You are thinking that I must earn my living," she replied. "That is something over which I too have been puzzling."

She paused before she said:

"I can speak several languages, and I can play the piano, but not well enough to be a professional. I can ride any horse, however obstreperous, and when I have to do so, I can sew."

She gave a little laugh before she added:

"It is not a very impressive list of accomplishments considering the years I have spent reading and learning. In fact, I am rather ashamed of it."

The Marquis did not reply.

He was thinking that all those things were admirable in a young lady of leisure, but none of them would be likely to enable Lucia to earn any money.

Then she said:

"I forgot to add that I can cook, and Papa was particular about what he ate. But I do not suppose anybody would employ me in their kitchens."

The idea of Lucia slaving over a hot stove or struggling to maintain authority over the scullions, who the Marquis had always thought were a rough lot, was ludicrous, and he said:

"It would obviously be impossible for you to take a menial job of any sort."

"I do not know why you should say that," she replied. "I looked after Papa, and naturally I had to clean the rooms in which we lived, and cook for him, when we could afford the food."

"I think you are arguing for the sake of argument," the Marquis said with a smile. "I will find you something far more congenial than that. You can leave it to me."

"I have not yet ... thanked you for ... Papa's Funeral, which I ... left to you," Lucia said in a low voice. "It was very ... beautiful ... and very ... competently done."

She was silent. Then she said with a note of pain in her voice:

"If it had not been for you, he would have had a pauper's grave, and that would have been horrifying and shaming."

"But I was there," the Marquis added, "and, as you have already said, I arrived at just the right time, so it was obviously meant to be. Therefore, stop worrying about what you would have done if things had been different."

"I must try," Lucia agreed meekly.

Once again she was looking ahead, and the Marquis, seeing her perfect profile against the water, thought that Beaumont must have been, as he had looked, extremely well bred.

He tried to remember if he had known any Beaumonts but could not recall anybody of that name.

'When I get a chance, I will talk to her about her family,' he thought, 'but this is not the right moment.'

He had expected her to wear black for her father's Funeral, although it was a very warm day, and the dark, drab, threadbare gown she was wearing when he had first seen her in the Piazza San Marco had been black.

But to his surprise she was wearing a gown of white

muslin which was not new and not expensive but in good taste.

Her bonnet was trimmed with white ribbons, and as if Lucia knew he was looking at her in surprise when she had come into the room where he was waiting for her, she had said:

"I . . . I hope you will not think it very . . . strange that I am not wearing . . . black for Papa . . . but it is something he greatly disliked."

The Marquis had raised his eye-brows, and she had continued:

"He did not believe in death. To him, everything was alive, which was why he painted as he did . . . and when Mama . . . died, he would not let me wear anything . . . black because he said it was an . . . insult to our belief that we would see her again."

The Marquis felt he had never heard anything appertaining to the Next World expressed so well.

Although he had often doubted whether Heaven or Hell existed, and whether there was any life to come after the one he was living now, he thought the way Lucia spoke was very touching.

So he had said what he knew she would expect:

"I am sure your father was right, and may I say that I am certain you look exactly as he would have wished you to on such a lovely day."

"I thought . . . you would . . . understand," she had said softly.

Then she had walked down the stairs beside him to where the gondola was waiting for them.

Now as they moved on towards the Grand Canal, the Marquis found himself thinking how lovely she would look if she were dressed by one of the great gownmakers who dressed the beauties in London as if they were Queens.

He felt that he would like to see Lucia, entirely from an artistic point of view, in gowns of silk and satin embroidered with silver or gold, and with wreaths of flowers in her hair and decorating the hems of her gowns.

He was quite certain that even as she was, her beauty would attract attention simply because she was so different.

But he decided that if she was well dressed she would be a sensation and would eclipse any of the "Incomparables" or the Social Beauties in the *Beau Monde*.

Then he wondered if he was being beguiled by her and the background of Venice, just as her father's paintings had beguiled him in a way that perhaps nobody else would appreciate.

As if she knew he was thinking about her, Lucia turned to look at him and say:

"You have not... changed your mind... My Lord? You would not... prefer me to leave in a ship for England... rather than... incommode you by staying with... you in your *Palazzo*?"

"I have already told you that it does not incommode me," the Marquis replied, "and I have every intention of taking you safely to England. I have a feeling, Lucia, that you will not be able to manage by yourself."

She gave a little shiver and said:

"It would be very... very frightening. At the same time... I have been thinking that now that I have lost both Papa and Mama, I must learn to be efficient... and you are quite... right to say that I must find... employment of some sort."

"I should not have brought up the subject," the Marquis said, "because we have a great deal to talk about first, and it will be some time before we reach England."

"Nevertheless, the question is there," Lucia said in a practical manner, "and I must think about what I can do, and prepare myself to do it."

She was silent for a moment. Then, almost as if she was speaking to herself, she said:

"I had very intelligent teachers to educate me. Mama would not employ a Governess because she said she was always sorry for them as they never seemed to fit in."

"I suppose that is true," the Marquis agreed, "but I think, Lucia, you are too young to be a Governess."

"Perhaps that is so, but I had a much better education than most Governesses have."

She thought he looked at her sceptically, and she said:

"Papa was very insistent that I should be as well read and as knowledgeable as both he and Mama were. He gained a degree at Oxford, and Mama was so clever that Papa wanted her to write a book."

"Why did she not do so?"

Lucia gave a little laugh.

"She said she refused to waste time which she could spend with Papa and me, but I think if Papa had died first, that is what she would have done."

"What would she have written about?"

"There were dozens of subjects on which she was very knowledgeable, such as philosophy, the native customs of Europe, and the inferior position that women occupy all over the world."

The Marquis was astounded.

"How could your mother know about such things?" he enquired.

To his surprise, instead of giving him an explanation, Lucia looked away from him, and, as had happened once before, a faint flush crept up her pale cheeks.

He was aware without her saying so that she thought she had said too much, and instead of answering his question, she said:

"I think the Grand Canal looks more beautiful from here than from any other place."

What she said was indeed true, because from there the long curving line of high *Palazzos* led to the Rialto Bridge, which hundreds of artists had painted.

The Marquis was just about to complain that she was evading his question, when he thought that it would be a mistake to upset her today when she had already passed through such an emotional experience as her father's Funeral.

Instead, he agreed with what she had said, and a few minutes later they arrived at his *Palazzo*.

They went up the stairs, and Lucia went at once to her bedroom to take off her bonnet.

It was some time before she joined the Marquis in the attractive Library where he had hung her father's paintings.

He was standing looking at one of them, finding once again that the light which Beaumont had depicted on the water and sky seemed almost to vibrate towards him, when Lucia came into the room.

She walked to his side to say very quietly:

"That is my favourite of all Papa's paintings. I thought when he had finished it that it was speaking to me."

"That is what I was thinking myself," the Marquis replied.

She flashed him a little glance that told him once again that she thought him wonderful because he understood, and he saw that she had been crying.

However, he made no comment, but as he sat down on the sofa he said:

"I have ordered an English tea which I am sure you will appreciate, unless of course you would prefer a glass of champagne?"

"I would much rather have tea," Lucia answered.

Although the *Palazzo* could not supply the sort of silver to which the Marquis was accustomed, he appreciated the way the Chef had made sandwiches and cakes in what was considered the English style.

Lucia poured out the tea, and he noticed that she did so with the same grace and ease as he would have expected of any Lady of Quality.

Tea-making had become almost a sacred rite in England since the reign of Queen Anne, and the Marquis had often found himself irritated by the women whom he had under his protection, who bungled the task.

However, Lucia's performance was faultless, and as she sipped the China tea which the Marquis knew had been brought with them in his yacht as a precaution, she very delicately ate first a small sandwich, then a piece of cake.

He looked at the number of dishes which were filled with delicacies and said:

"Unless you wish to appear too thin to be fashionable, you will have to make a greater effort at eating than you are at this moment!"

Lucia gave a little laugh.

"I have never eaten so much in my life, not even when I was at home."

"You must tell me about your home," the Marquis said. "You have already said your father sold everything you possessed before he left England, but I presume you have some relatives who will be only too pleased to welcome you when you return."

There was a silence. Then Lucia replied:

"You . . . said we would not . . . talk about it now."

"There is of course no hurry," the Marquis agreed, "but at the same time, I think you would be wise to write to an aunt or cousin, or grandparent, and tell them your circumstances, so that they may be prepared for your arrival."

Lucia looked down at her plate, and as the Marquis watched her he thought that against the walls of the Library she looked very young and frail.

Perhaps it was just the impression she made with the fairness of her hair and the translucent whiteness of her skin, but he felt that she was far too insubstantial to cope with anything, including her own future.

Then he told himself that he was being ridiculous.

She was thin from lack of food and from nursing her father, but otherwise she was doubtless a healthy young woman, and it was his duty to make her face up to what lay ahead of her.

Then, as if she realised he was waiting for an answer to his question, she said:

"You will . . . think it very strange . . . but I . . . have no relatives!"

"What do you mean—you have no relatives? Everybody has relatives, whether they like them or not!"

"Unfortunately, I have . . . none!"

Now she spoke firmly and in a manner that indicated that the subject was closed, and the Marquis stared at her almost in consternation.

"I cannot believe that is true."

There was silence. Then Lucia said:

"I have already said that I do not wish to be an . . . encumbrance to Your Lordship. You were kind enough to say you would . . . take me to England, and when I get . . . there, I will find . . . somewhere to . . . go."

"Now you are being ridiculous and secretive," the Marquis said angrily. "You know perfectly well that I cannot accept such a statement."

"I will . . . manage."

The Marquis frowned.

"I know you are counting on the money I am paying you for your father's paintings," he said, "but you must be aware that it will not last forever. What is more, a girl of your age and with your looks cannot wander about alone. It is quite impossible!"

"I shall be safe enough," Lucia said, "because I will go . . . back to . . . Little Morden."

"Even though the house has been sold?"

"There is somebody with whom I can stay."

"Whom?"

He thought she had no wish to tell him, but after a moment, as if he compelled her to do so, she replied reluctantly:

"My old Nanny, whom I had when I was a child, has a cottage in the village."

The Marquis looked at Lucia as if he thought she could not be telling him the truth or else was putting on an act for his benefit.

Then as he looked into her eyes, he knew she could not lie without his being aware of it, and said:

"That is hardly a feasible plan for more than a few weeks. You cannot expect to spend the rest of your life in Little Morden."

"I shall be . . . safe there."

He knew the word meant a great deal to her.

As if there was no more to be said on the subject, she asked:

"May I pour you out another cup of tea, My Lord?"

When he refused, she poured some more tea into her own cup.

She had just picked it up when the door of the Library was flung open and a vision in silks and feathers and jewels appeared.

It was Francesca, and as the Marquis rose slowly to his feet, he realised from the manner of her entrance and the expression in her eyes that she was in one of her more dramatic moods.

He had had so much to think about since bringing Lucia back to the *Palazzo* after her father's death, and arranging Beaumont's Funeral, that he had almost forgotten Francesca.

Now it flashed through his mind that she must have been extremely annoyed that he had not attended the Opera last night, nor had he taken her out to supper as she would have expected.

However, before dining alone with Lucia in the *Palazzo*, he had sent a note to the Theatre apologising to Francesca for being unable to entertain her as he had hoped to do.

He had told Mr. Johnson to see that the messenger took a large basket of orchids with the note.

He had then more or less forgotten Francesca as he had talked to Lucia over dinner, and found himself intrigued and in fact enthralled by how much she knew about painting and pictures and artists.

She had not exaggerated when she had said she was well read. He had quoted Joachim du Bellay, the most magical of the poets of the French Renaissance, in French:

"Their superb arsenal, their ships, their landings,
Their Saint Mark, their Palace, their Rialto, their
poetry."

and she had capped with Wordsworth's sonnet:

*"Men are we, and must grieve when even the Shade
Of that which once was great is passed away."*

He was aware that her knowledge came from her
father, but the Marquis, who was fascinated by detail, had
found what she told him was so absorbing that they had
talked until he realised he was being almost cruel in
keeping her awake so late.

He had therefore sent her to bed.

But because his mind felt stimulated and he was
therefore not tired, he had ordered a gondola and told the
gondolier to take him out onto the Grand Canal.

It had been a night of stars and magic and, as the
Venetians would undoubtedly have thought, one of romance.

The Marquis did not mind being alone.

He had a great deal to think about, and it had been a
relief not to have to listen to the chatter of voices or the
artificial laughter which he knew would have been very
much part of the supper-party to which he should have
taken Francesca.

He had not given a thought all evening to the Teatro
la Fenice with its gilt and pink plush auditorium under a
ceiling rioting with cherubs.

He should have sat in a Box with a bunch of scarlet
carnations on its balcony, and in the Boxes on either side
of him beautiful women would have been a blaze of
diamonds.

Symbolic red, white, and green bouquets would have
been thrown on the stage at the end of Francesca's performance, and occasionally there would have been one
tied with the Austrian colours for the pleasure of watching
her kick it scornfully aside.

Instead, content and at ease, the Marquis had stayed
on the lagoon so late that when he had returned to the
Palazzo, he learnt from a servant that Francesca had
returned several hours earlier and would now be asleep.

He had no wish to awaken her and was only relieved to think that she would make no demands on him.

Instead, he had gone to bed alone and slept peacefully, to awaken early, as usual, and once again, as he had done the day before, he had gone for a walk because he needed the exercise.

This time there was no Lucia to come to his side when he had finished his walk and stopped for a cup of coffee at Florian's.

When he returned home, Mr. Johnson was waiting to inform him about the arrangements for the Funeral, then he had left him to tell Lucia when it would take place.

He was relieved to find on his return that Francesca had left for another rehearsal, and he had therefore not seen her today until this moment.

After her dramatic pause in the doorway as if making an entrance on the stage and making sure of the audience's attention, she walked towards him. But as she did so, her eyes were not on him but on Lucia.

"I heard you had another guest!"

It was not a statement but an accusation.

"Good-day, Francesca!" the Marquis said. "May I introduce to you an Englishwoman whose father, as I expect you have heard, was a very talented artist, but who has most sadly died."

"How convenient that you, My Lord, were here to comfort her!" Francesca remarked sarcastically.

The Marquis was aware that she was about to be difficult.

Quickly, because he wanted to avoid a scene, he said:

"You must have had a very tiring rehearsal. Will you have some tea? Or may I offer you a glass of champagne?"

"I do not want anything but an explanation!" Francesca retorted. "How could you have neglected me last night by omitting to give me supper as you had promised? Then when I returned you were not here."

She almost spat the last words at him, and the Marquis realised that whenever he was not in the *Palazzo*, she would be quite certain in her mind that wherever he was, he was not alone.

Beginning to feel annoyed at the way in which she was confronting him, he replied:

"I suggest we discuss this, Francesca, when we are alone."

Because she felt embarrassed, Lucia rose to her feet and said:

"I will ... go to my ... room, My Lord."

"*Your* room?" Francesca questioned shrilly. "And I suppose it is now *your Palazzo*, and the Marquis, being *your* lover, has no further use for me!"

Her voice rose hysterically, and Lucia looked at her wide-eyed as if she was mesmerised.

She was so bemused by the singer's appearance and the way she spoke that although she had risen to her feet to leave, she was still holding in her hand the cup from which she had been drinking.

Now the Marquis said sharply:

"There is no need for you to leave, Lucia. *Signorina* Rosso and I will talk elsewhere."

He spoke so firmly that Lucia remained staring at Francesca.

"I have no intention of talking to you anywhere, My Lord, but here!" Francesca declared. "I want an explanation. What have I done? What could I have said? And why have you changed?"

She threw out her arms dramatically as she said:

"I am forgotten—neglected. I have not even the consolation of wearing the necklace you promised me. I thought an Englishman never broke his word!"

She was being over-dramatic and acting as she might have done on a stage.

As she spoke, the Marquis knew that the whole crux of the situation rested on two things: that he had not come to her room to make love to her last night as she had expected, and that the emerald necklace had not yet materialised.

Coldly and with an icy note in his voice which Alastair would have known showed that his temper was rising, he replied:

"I do not break my word, Francesca. The necklace I promised you shall be yours, but as I do not like being browbeaten in my own house, I suggest you would be very much more comfortable in your own apartment."

Francesca gave a scream that seemed to echo round the walls.

"Are you daring to turn me out?"

"I am thinking only of your comfort," the Marquis replied, "which I have obviously failed to provide."

Francesca gave another scream and came closer to him so that they faced each other across the small tea-table.

"If you dare to do this to me—Francesca Rosso—you will be sorry!" she said. "I have never been so insulted by any man."

"I am sorry if you feel like that, Francesca," the Marquis replied, "but I must beg of you to end this very uncomfortable tirade. If you will not come and talk to me sensibly in another room, then it would be best for me to leave you alone to recover from your quite unnecessary anger."

He made a movement as if he would walk away, but he had no intention of leaving Francesca and Lucia alone.

Francesca made a gesture to stop him.

"You will not leave me!" she said. "I will not be made the laughing-stock of Venice because you have no further use for me! You shall pay—yes, My Lord—you shall pay for what you have done to a woman who gave you her heart!"

As she spoke, her voice rising almost to a scream of anger, she put her hand down the front of her low bodice and swiftly drew out a long, thin stiletto.

As it gleamed in the light coming from the window there was something very evil about it.

She raised it with a flamboyant gesture that she had

used a hundred times upon the stage, aiming it with all her strength at the Marquis's heart.

Because it was something he had never anticipated in his wildest dreams, he was for the moment frozen into immobility.

But as Lucia, watching, realised what the Venetian was about to do, instantly and without thinking she threw the contents of the cup she held into Francesca's face.

The hot tea blinded her eyes, diverting the blow which she intended to inflict on the Marquis—and which might easily have killed him—to pierce the cloth of his coat just below the shoulder.

At the same time, as if the Marquis came to his senses, he reached out to catch Francesca's wrist in his right hand and force her to drop the stiletto to the floor.

She gave first a scream of pain from the vise-like grip of his fingers, then went into hysterics as she sank down on a chair, screaming, laughing, and crying all at the same time.

Lucia stood with the empty cup in her hand, unable to breathe. It was then that the Marquis said in a quiet voice:

"Go to your room, Lucia!"

She put down the cup.

"You are . . . wounded!"

"It is nothing. Only a scratch. Do as I tell you."

He could barely make himself heard above the noise Francesca was making, but Lucia understood.

As if she was too frightened to stay, and at the same time was escaping from something ugly and unpleasant, she ran from the room with the swiftness of a small animal seeking shelter.

The Marquis waited until she was out of sight. Then he said sharply:

"Behave yourself, Francesca! I am appalled at your behaviour, and if you had killed me you would have caused an international incident which would certainly have ruined your career."

Francesca pressed her lips together, then said in a different tone:

"How can you be so cruel to me? You have broken my heart!"

"I daresay the present I will give you, if you behave yourself, will more than adequately repair it."

The Marquis spoke coldly and in a firm voice that proclaimed more clearly than words his distaste of what had occurred.

Then, as if Francesca regretted that she had lost control of her feelings, she said with an exaggerated humility:

"Forgive me! It is because I love you and cannot bear to lose you to any other woman that I could not conceal my unhappiness."

"I hardly think that justifies what might have been murder," the Marquis answered.

As he spoke he picked up the stiletto from the floor and walking to the open window flung it out into the Canal.

Then he walked to the fireplace to ring for a servant.

Francesca sat still, her eyes watching him.

Then slowly she took off her feather-trimmed bonnet and smoothed her dark hair into place.

The door opened and the Marquis said:

"*Signorina* Rosso has to leave immediately! Have her belongings packed, and they can follow her in another gondola."

The Marquis spoke in Italian, and the servant bowed his head to show that he understood, then shut the door.

Francesca waited a moment. Then she sprang to her feet and ran to the Marquis to fling her arms round his neck.

"Pardon me," she begged. "I love you with all my heart. You cannot send me away! I swear I will die if you do!"

The Marquis unlocked her hands from behind his neck.

"It is no use, Francesca," he said. "You are shrewd enough to realise that when the curtain falls there is nothing you can do about it. I will give you some money now!"

He paused to say more slowly:

"Whether or not I give you the necklace before I leave Venice will depend on your behaviour. Any more scenes or attempts at assassination such as that which has just taken place, and the necklace will not be bought."

Francesca knew she was beaten, and with a flounce she walked away from him towards the window, saying vehemently:

"I hate you!"

The Marquis smiled cynically but did not reply.

Instead he sat down at the desk and wrote a cheque which he knew was large enough to pacify the greediest demands of the singer.

He walked across the room to hand it to her, and watching the expression in her eyes he knew that she was surprised that it was such a large amount.

"I do not suppose you wish me to thank you?" she asked.

He knew she was still wondering in her crafty mind whether there was any chance of enticing him once again to become her lover.

He had heard of her outbursts of uncontrollable bad temper in the Theatre, and he realised that she had acted spontaneously and without considering the consequences and was now deeply regretting losing such a rich protector.

He looked at her, thinking it was a pity that her undoubted beauty should be spoilt by a temperament over which she had no control.

"You must learn to act, Francesca," he said, "off the stage as well as on, and you should be grateful that anything so prosaic as a cup of tea has saved you from being taken at this moment to the prison in Venice, which reputedly is not a very comfortable place."

Francesca shrugged her shoulders, but there was no doubt that she was now regretting what she had done.

There was a droop at the corners of her red mouth, her eyes were dark, and there was an expression of dismay in them when only a short time ago they had been fiery with anger and passion.

The Marquis lifted her hand to his lips.

"Good-bye, Francesca," he said. "Thank you for the happy times we have had together, and remember in the future to keep that temper of yours under control as if it were a savage beast."

Francesca gave what was quite a realistic little sob.

"I do not wish to lose you," she said. "And what am I to say when I am laughed at for having done so?"

"You can tell them the truth," the Marquis answered, "that I am returning to England, because that is exactly what I am doing."

"You are really going?"

"Immediately!" he said. "There is nothing to keep me here any longer."

He let go of her hand, and although she tried to hold on to him, he turned away.

"The gondola will be waiting for you, Francesca," he said, and walked from the Library, leaving her alone.

Francesca made a movement as if she would follow him, then as she realised it was hopeless, she stamped her foot.

"How can I have been so foolish?" she asked. "Fool! Fool! Fool! That is me!"

Then, knowing she must accept the inevitable, she picked up her bonnet from where she had placed it on a chair and put it on her dark head.

There was a gold-framed mirror hanging on one wall and she stood in front of it, arranging her curls on either side of her pretty, painted face.

Then as she looked at her reflection she smiled, and her eyes seemed to sparkle at the same time.

"If he is leaving, I shall have the emerald necklace tomorrow," she told herself.

Then with her head held high and walking with the acquired grace with which she moved about the stage, she went from the Library to be escorted down the stairs by one of the servants to where the gondola was waiting for her.

* * *

By the time she reached her bedroom, Lucia was trembling.

She had never in her life believed that any woman could behave in the way that Francesca had done, or could threaten a man with a weapon which Lucia knew only too well would have injured the Marquis dangerously if it had not actually killed him.

Her father had often talked to her about the stilettoes which the Italians used in their feuds and fights with one another despite the danger involved in using them.

"We think duelling is dangerous," he had said, "but I assure you that stilettoes are the invention of the devil! I once saw a big man die after being stabbed with a stiletto by an opponent who was far smaller and frailer than he was."

He added disparagingly:

"He would not have lasted one round had they been boxing with each other."

The way her father had talked about stilettoes had made Lucia hope that she would never see one being used.

And yet she knew now that she had been able to save the Marquis not only because of what he had told her but because her instinct had warned her that the Venetian woman was in a murderous rage.

Even to think of the long, thin, evil knife embedded in his heart made her feel sick and frightened her to the point where her hands were cold and she was shivering.

She sat down on the edge of the bed and put her face in her hands.

She could not bear to think of the Marquis dying in such a horrible way.

Then she remembered that if she had lost him, on top of her father's death, she would now be completely alone in the world and perhaps unable to obtain the money he had promised to pay for the paintings.

It was wrong, she knew, to think of herself when the Marquis had been in danger, but she was shaken besides being appalled by what had just occurred.

She had not lived in Venice for two years without knowing that at the slightest excuse the Venetians became intensely dramatic.

They dramatised everything until, with their eyes flashing and their hands gesticulating, they seemed to be eternally in a passion about something, and Lucia had in fact become quite used to their outbursts.

But she had never believed it possible that any woman would attempt to kill a man, especially one whom she professed to love.

She had of course heard of Francesca Rosso, and although she had been to the Opera with her father and mother in the past, they had not been able to afford it recently, so she had not heard her sing.

It was to be expected, because she was so beautiful and so young to be a Prima Donna, that there would be men to admire her and, Lucia thought, undoubtedly to love her for herself.

The Marquis had not told her that Francesca was staying at the *Palazzo*, and because he had said there would be no other guests and she had not seen anybody, it had not occurred to Lucia that they were anything but alone.

Now for the first time she thought it strange that he had not explained Francesca's presence, and she was also suddenly aware that because he was the Prima Donna's lover, he was a—man.

The Marquis had been right when he had thought that to Lucia he was not a man, and an attractive one as other women had found him, but a supernatural being who had appeared from the sky or from Olympus at exactly the right moment to save her and her father.

Now as Lucia sat on her bed with her hands over her face, she was seeing the Marquis in a new and very different light.

Because of it, she suddenly felt embarrassed that she had cried in his arms when her father had died and had allowed him to bring her here unchaperoned.

She was sure that her mother would have expected her to be accompanied by another woman if she was to stay in his house.

She could hardly visualise that he intended Francesca to be a Chaperone.

Yet, if she demanded one now, perhaps he would turn her away as he had rid himself of the singer, and would not take her to England with him.

"What is the right thing for me to do, Mama?" Lucia asked.

Then she told herself that she was being ridiculous.

How could she, penniless and orphaned, expect the Marquis to treat her as if she were a Society girl?

She was just a stray beggar he had picked up in the street and to whom he had extended his kindness.

Of course she need not be chaperoned, because as far as he was concerned she was nothing in his life.

Why should she be anything else, considering that he had someone as attractive and exciting as Francesca Rosso as his mistress?

It had been impossible for Lucia to live in Venice without realising that the Venetians paid little attention to their wives, and most of the aristocrats spent their time with their mistresses.

Everywhere she went with her father and mother she had seen them travelling in the gondolas, moving about the *Piazzas*, coming out of the Restaurants, or sitting in the Opera Boxes rouged and bejewelled, and looking resplendent, alluring, and inviting, but certainly not respectable.

She supposed she should not have been surprised that the Marquis should have taken the most talked of Prima Donna in Venice for his mistress, and having seen Francesca Rosso she could understand her attractions only too well.

Never had she imagined that any woman could be so beautiful and at the same time look so unconventional.

It was one thing to be painted and rouged on the stage, but Francesca's whole appearance when she came into the Library had been so sensational and so theatrical that Lucia had found herself mesmerised.

Then when she started to quarrel with the Marquis and had become more and more dramatic and hysterical, Lucia had felt it impossible to move or even to breathe.

She felt that somehow, by some mischance, she had stepped onto the stage and become part of a play which was being performed.

"She would have killed him!" she told herself now.

Just as Francesca had done, she wanted to scream at the very idea.

There was a knock on the door, and thinking it was a servant, Lucia took her hands from her face, rose to her feet, and tried to appear composed before she said:

"Come . . . in!"

As the door opened she saw that it was the Marquis.

For a moment she could only look at him, her eyes seeming to fill her whole face, and he knew from her expression and the movement of her hands what she was feeling.

There was silence between them before he said quietly:

"I have come to tell you, Lucia, that we are leaving for England immediately. I have ordered the gondolas to take us to the yacht, and we will stay there tonight. I will arrange for our belongings to be packed up and brought aboard before daylight so that we can leave at dawn."

He spoke impersonally, as if he were giving orders to one of his staff.

Then, as she did not answer, he said:

"I will wait for you in the Salon, and we will have a glass of champagne before we leave. Do not keep me waiting!"

He shut the door, and Lucia stood still after he had gone, just staring at it.

Then she knew that she had no decisions to make. The Marquis had made them for her.

All she had to do was to obey—but that would not stop her from thinking.

Chapter Five

The Marquis was waiting in the Salon when Lucia came somewhat nervously from her bedroom.

She appreciated that he had not asked her to return to the Library from which she had fled in consternation.

She saw as she entered the very beautiful room, with its high-backed chairs covered in needle-point and tapestries covering most of the walls, that he had changed his coat which had been damaged by the stiletto.

Otherwise, he was still wearing the clothes he had worn to her father's Funeral.

She glanced at him, then glanced away, and as if he realised how shy and embarrassed she was, he said in a calm, matter-of-fact voice:

"I am looking forward to showing you my yacht."

As he spoke he handed her a glass of champagne, and picking up his own lifted it high in his hand.

"Let us drink to a calm voyage home!"

Obediently Lucia raised her glass, then took a little sip from it.

"You told me," the Marquis went on, "that you can ride an obstreperous horse, and I am hoping that *The Sea Horse* will not be too obstreperous for you."

"I . . . was not . . . seasick on the . . . way here," Lucia said in a faltering little voice.

"I was going to ask you if you came by sea or land," the Marquis answered. "Personally, I prefer the sea."

Lucia felt that was what she would have expected him to say.

She knew that everybody who did the "Grand Tour" spoke of the long hours of boredom when the horses were climbing the mountain-passes slowly, and the wheels of their carriages became embedded with mud and had to be dug out.

The Marquis finished his champagne and put down the glass.

"I know it will please you to learn that I have given strict instructions to my secretary," he said, "that your father's paintings should be packed with the greatest care and they are to be the first thing taken on board."

Lucia had already realised that because the Marquis had suddenly announced that he was returning home, it had put a tremendous strain on the staff.

She had been aware since she had been staying at the *Palazzo* how much he had brought with him from England.

All the sheets on the beds, the towels, the tableclothes, and the napkins bore his monogram surmounted by a coronet, and the gold ornaments on the table at dinner were engraved with his crest. The champagne, too, and other French wines had been brought from England.

A number of the servants in the *Palazzo* were English, and Lucia knew they were His Lordship's personal staff.

She imagined that she could hear everybody already bustling in and out of the great rooms, knowing that if their Master had said they were leaving at dawn, he would be extremely incensed if they were unable to do so.

He was waiting for her, and she took another sip of her champagne.

"Shall we go?" he asked.

"Yes . . . of course," she answered, rising to her feet.

She had the feeling that he was eager not only to return to England but even more to escape from Venice, and she could understand that he had no wish to see the tempestuous Prima Donna again.

Then, as if she remembered how he had been injured, she asked quickly:

"Is your arm . . . all right?"

"A mere scratch," the Marquis replied loftily.

"But have you had it washed and dressed?" Lucia asked. "Even a scratch can be dangerous unless you are very careful."

"I will see to it when I get to the yacht."

He walked towards the door, and there was nothing Lucia could do but follow him.

Then as they went down the stairs he said:

"I have a feeling you are worrying about me, but there is no need."

"There is every need," Lucia argued. "Supposing anything should . . . happen to you?"

The Marquis smiled.

"Are you thinking of me or of yourself?"

For a moment she was embarrassed by his question, then she replied:

"If I am truthful . . . both!"

The Marquis laughed.

"That was not the answer I expected, and I therefore commend you, Lucia, on being that most unusual phenomenon—a woman who actually tells the truth!"

Lucia did not reply, and the Marquis found that once again he could read her thoughts. He knew she was thinking that he must have known some very strange women.

Then he told himself that having lived in the quiet of the country with her father and mother, she had no idea of the prevarications, evasions, intrigues, and downright lies which were employed by Ladies of Society.

Where those of the other world were concerned, deception was part of their profession and their stock-in-trade.

Only as the gondola was moving quickly down the Grand Canal did he wonder how Lucia's presence would affect his journey home.

He had the idea that it might be very different from the time he had spent alone on his voyage to Venice.

Then he looked at her and thought that in the plain white gown she had worn all day with a shawl round her shoulders, she looked so lovely that he found it hard to believe her beauty was real.

"Perhaps she is just part of Venice," he told himself, "and like an exotic flower will not transplant into another environment."

Then he remembered that she was English, at least so she had said, but there was something about her which told him that that was not the whole truth.

As if she was aware that he was thinking of her, Lucia turned to look at him with a question in her eyes, and he asked:

"Are you saying good-bye to Venice?"

"I am trying to . . . remember what Papa . . . said about it. If he were here, he would say we must . . . look at the . . . light."

There was no doubt that as it was late in the afternoon the strange apricot tinge that the Marquis had noticed before seemed to colour the last of the two hundred palaces on the Grand Canal and tint the waters of the lagoon.

He remembered somebody had once said that one of the peculiarities of the light in Venice was that its intensity derived as much from the horizon as from the sun.

Now as he looked towards the horizon he wondered if Alastair would think he had reached new horizons in his mind and perhaps, to put it poetically, opened new windows to his soul.

Then he laughed mockingly at himself and thought that nothing was changed.

Only Francesca had behaved a little more outrageously than some of the other women he had taken under his protection, and all he had acquired from Venice were six paintings by an unknown artist.

Then as Lucia made a little movement with one of her

hands, he told himself cynically that he could add her to the list.

At the quay-side there were a number of ships from different lands, and as they neared his yacht the Marquis thought that it stood out like a well-bred stallion amongst a lot of very inferior horses.

He had designed it for speed, having taken as a model the American pirate ships which had preyed during their war with the British on the cargo vessels and proved themselves superior to any other ship at sea.

The Admiralty had captured one and made the Ship-builders study it with care.

The Marquis, realising how revolutionary it was as a sea-going vessel, had, immediately the war with Napoleon ended, ordered a private yacht to be built on the American lines.

The Sea Horse evoked the admiration and envy of every ship-owner wherever he took it, and now he was not surprised to find that there was quite a crowd on the quay as he and Lucia went aboard.

His Captain saluted them, and the Marquis said:

"I expect you received my message, Captain Bateson. I wish to leave for England as soon as possible, but obviously we have to wait for the luggage to be brought aboard, and that will take a little time."

"I've already, at Mr. Johnson's request, M'Lord, sent six of the crew to the *Palazzo* to help those already there."

"Thank you, Captain."

The Marquis guided Lucia down into the Saloon.

As soon as she saw it she realised that *The Sea Horse* was very different from any ship she had ever seen or imagined.

To begin with, it was exquisitely decorated, and the Saloon itself was more like an English Drawing-Room than anything she had expected to find in a sea-going vessel.

There were fine paintings on the walls, curtains to cover the port-holes, and the sofa and chairs were in an attractive green material.

She looked round, and the Marquis watched her face before he asked:

"Well? What is your verdict?"

She smiled at him before she answered:

"Need you ask? It is beautiful and quite different from what I expected."

"What did you expect?"

"I suppose something austere and very practical."

"I was thinking more of my guests than myself when I designed this."

She imagined he was referring to the fact that he would be entertaining beautiful women, and as she thought again of Francesca Rosso the colour rose in her cheeks.

"Forget her!" the Marquis said quietly. "That chapter is finished, and now we turn the page to begin another one."

Lucia smiled to show that she understood what he was saying. Then with a little cry she exclaimed:

"But first, before we think of anything else, you must have your arm seen to. Although you will not admit it, I believe it is beginning to hurt you."

"You sound regrettably like a Nanny I once had," the Marquis answered, "but if it will prevent you from nagging me, you had better come to my cabin and prove your skill in taking away the pain."

They walked from the Saloon, and when Lucia saw the Master Cabin she was even more impressed.

It took up the whole stern and was, she thought, exactly the cabin the Master of a ship should have.

There was a box-like bed with four carved posts, which her father had told her was the prerogative of every Admiral or Captain of a man-o'-war.

But apart from that, all the other furniture seemed to be fitted onto the walls so that even the roughest sea could not dislodge them.

There were several very attractive paintings by Maritime artists on the walls, a thick carpet on the floor, and two deep armchairs in which a man could relax.

As Lucia looked round, the Marquis took off his tight-fitting whip-cord coat.

When he did so, she gave a little cry, for there was a crimson stain on his white linen shirt.

The Marquis looked at it a little ruefully before he untied his cravat and pulled his shirt from his shoulder, saying:

"I was not aware when I changed my coat that I was bleeding."

Lucia inspected what was a long, unpleasant scratch where the point of the stiletto had slit the sleeve of his coat and across the top of his arm.

The wound was several inches long, and she knew that if she had not diverted Francesca's aim, the stiletto would have been buried in the Marquis's chest.

As if he was thinking the same thing, he asked:

"Well? What are you going to do about it?"

"Could I have a little brandy?"

The Marquis raised his eye-brows.

"Are you going to drink it, or am I?"

"Neither," she replied. "I am going to use it to clean the wound just in case it is infected. If it is, you will run a fever."

"Now you are trying to frighten me!"

"Mama was always insistent that any open wound could be dangerous unless it was kept clean. Actually, brandy was used for that purpose at the Battle of Trafalgar, and should have been used ten years later at Waterloo."

"I believe you are reproaching me for my ignorance," the Marquis remarked, "but I am quite prepared to bow to your superior knowledge."

As he spoke, he walked to the bed to pick up a gold bell which stood beside it.

He rang it sharply and a moment later the cabin door was opened.

"Come in, Evans," the Marquis said to his valet. "Miss Beaumont insists that I must use my best brandy to clean the wound on my arm."

"Wound, M'Lord?" Evans enquired. "What's Your Lordship been up to now?"

The Marquis smiled.

He was well aware that by this time, because Evans had been at the *Palazzo*, he would have learnt exactly what had happened and the way in which Francesca had behaved.

Nothing could ever be kept from the knowledge of the servants, and Evans, being over-protective, must have been horrified that any woman should behave in such a way towards his Master.

He had followed them from the *Palazzo* in another gondola, and now he said reproachfully:

"You didn't tell me, M'Lord, you wanted to change your coat. I were downstairs and couldn't believe Your Lordship was leaving so quickly."

"But I have," the Marquis said good-humouredly, "and now you had better do something about me."

"So I should think, M'Lord!" Evans said. "Miss Beaumont's right: that's a nasty cut and should be cleaned, otherwise we'll have Your Lordship suffering the deliriums of a madman!"

"I hope not," the Marquis protested.

Evans produced from a cupboard a bottle of brandy and poured a little of it into a glass.

Then, watched by Lucia, he dipped a clean white linen handkerchief into it before he dabbed it on the Marquis's wound.

Because the brandy made it sting, the Marquis tightened his lips, but he did not complain, and when the wound was cleaned to Evans's satisfaction, he turned to Lucia to say:

"Will you bandage 'is Lordship, Miss, or shall I?"

The Marquis was startled.

It was the first time he had ever known Evans to allow anybody else to have any part in caring for him, and the man was in fact absurdly jealous of any other servant.

Then with a slight twinkle in his eyes, he realised that

Evans was showing his disapproval of Francesca and her
behaviour by being pleasant to what he thought of as his
Master's "new interest."

"Oh, please, will you do it?" Lucia answered. "I can
bandage if necessary, but I am sure you are much more
competent than I am."

She was certainly being very tactful, the Marquis
thought, for Evans, having made the magnanimous gesture, would have been extremely annoyed if she had
accepted it.

He bandaged the Marquis's arm skilfully, having first
of all covered the wound with a linen pad in case it
continued to bleed, then applied a bandage which was just
tight enough not to slip but was in no way constricting.

"Thank you, Evans," the Marquis said. "And now,
while I change my shirt for another, I suggest you take
Miss Beaumont to her cabin. I imagine she would be most
comfortable in the Waterloo Room."

Lucia looked surprised at the name, but the Marquis
did not explain, and she merely followed the valet from
the Master Cabin into the one next door.

As soon as she entered it she understood why it was
called after the Battle in which the Marquis had been
decorated for gallantry.

There were three paintings in the room—two were of
the Battle and one was a portrait of the Duke of Wellington.

Evans looked at them with satisfaction.

"Brings back memories, Miss, to them as was there."

"Were you with His Lordship?"

"I were! And havin' to look after 'im then as I does
now. Brave as a lion 'e be, and never thinks of 'imself."

Lucia looked round at the large bed draped with blue
curtains and the fitted furniture which was almost the
same as that in the Master Cabin.

"You'll be comfortable 'ere, Miss," Evans said, "an'
your luggage shouldn't be long in comin'. It were bein'
packed as I leaves the *Palazzo*."

"Thank you, thank you very much."

When the valet had left her to return to the Marquis, she put her shawl down on the small armchair which just fitted into the cabin and began to take off her bonnet.

The cabin was certainly very different from the one she had occupied in the ship in which she had travelled with her father and mother to Venice.

That had been very austere and most uncomfortable, and there had been only one small port-hole and not two as she had now.

When she had got into her bunk at night, she felt almost as if she lay in a coffin.

Considering the fact that this was a ship that had been built for speed, there was a remarkable amount of room, and she thought how exciting it was to be travelling in such luxury, and with the Marquis.

She went to the port-hole to look out at the sun, which was sinking low on the horizon, leaving a last glitter of gold over the smooth water.

'I am glad to be leaving Venice,' she thought in her heart.

And yet it was in some ways an agony to know that she left not only her father but also her mother behind in the City of Light.

'Perhaps I should have stayed there to be near them,' she thought.

Then she remembered how frightened she was of being alone and of the men who spoke to her and followed her however hard she tried to avoid them.

'In England it will be different," she told herself reassuringly.

And yet that was frightening too, except that now that she was with the Marquis, he would help her and perhaps look after her.

Then she remembered the coldness of his voice when he had spoken to Francesca, and she knew that just as he could be charming, kindly, and sympathetic, he could also be hard and ruthless.

Looking out the port-hole, she clasped her hands together and prayed:

"Please...God...do not let me...bore him too quickly. Make him as kind to me as he is now. If I...lose him, I shall have...nobody, and I shall be...afraid."

She felt herself tremble.

Then, almost as if the light outside spoke to her, she had the feeling that both her father and mother were protecting her and helping her, and things would not be as bad as she anticipated.

She remembered how the Marquis had said to Francesca that he always kept his promises and that she should have the emerald necklace.

Therefore, he would certainly keep his promise and pay her for her father's paintings.

"I shall not go home empty-handed," she told herself, "and somehow he will think of...something I can do, and I will be...safe."

When she thought of it, she knew that if she had travelled back alone in one of the ships that were outside in the harbour, it would in fact have been terrifying.

Because she had been with her mother and father on the way out from England, she had not worried about the other passengers.

She had known, however, that when she walked round the deck with her parents, men of every age had looked at her in a way which made her feel shy.

Her mother had therefore refused to be friendly with some of the people who approached them, even though she was always polite.

One evening, when they thought she was not listening, Lucia had heard her mother say to her father:

"In a few years' time Lucia will be very lovely, and we shall have to be very careful of her."

"She is only a child," her father replied.

"Children grow up, darling," her mother answered, "and I can only pray that Lucia will find a wonderful man like you to marry her and live happily ever afterwards."

"Is that what you have done?" her father asked.

"You know that ever since our marriage I have lived in Heaven!"

"With no regrets?"

"How can you ask anything so foolish?" her mother replied. "How could I regret being in Heaven with the most handsome magical, adorable man who ever existed?"

"That is what I want you to say, and you know that I am more blessed than any man could be in having you."

Her father and mother had looked into each other's eyes and Lucia knew she was forgotten.

Then as they went into their cabin and shut the door, she knew her father would be holding her mother close in his arms, and kissing her as if he would never let her go.

'That is what I want in my life,' she thought.

Then she felt despairingly that perhaps it would never happen and she would always be alone and afraid.

* * *

Very early the next morning Lucia was awakened by the sound of the anchor being raised and movements overhead.

She knew then that everything must have come aboard and they were now leaving Venice.

It had been an unexpected joy last night to sit in the attractive Saloon with the Marquis, waited on by stewards in white coats embellished with crested silver buttons rather than the elaborate livery which the servants had worn in the *Palazzo*.

The food as usual had been delicious, and the Marquis had insisted upon her having a glass of wine.

When they were alone he had said:

"I want to commend you, Lucia, on the exemplary manner in which you behaved today, which I admire in a way which is difficult to put into words."

He paused, as she looked shy and blushed a little, before he went on:

"I also want to thank you for saving my life."

"No... please..." Lucia began, but he interrupted:

"We will not speak of it again, but I just wanted to say that the quickness with which you acted was exceptional, and because if you had not done so the consequences might have been very serious, I can only say thank you from the bottom of my heart."

Then, as if he knew she was finding it embarrassing to reply, he said:

"Now I want you to tell me what you think of the paintings I have here in *The Sea Horse*."

He smiled as he added:

"It gave me a great deal of enjoyment to find them, especially those in this room, and tomorrow I will show you the other cabins, all of which I have named after the battles in which I took part."

"I am sure it is a very original idea," Lucia said.

"That is what the Duke of Wellington said when I told him that I not only had his portrait in my ship, but am having arranged in my house in London a room dedicated to him and the battles in which I served under him."

"That will be very interesting to anyone who is privileged to see it," Lucia said.

"It is certainly something that will keep me occupied," the Marquis answered, "and I intend to make a journey to France specifically to find pictures painted during the war by French artists."

"People must never forget how much England suffered in the years they fought Napoleon," Lucia said as if she spoke to herself. "But now that the war is over, there are so many other things to be done."

The Marquis looked surprised before he asked:

"What do you mean by that?"

Lucia hesitated a moment before she said:

"Mama and I always read the Parliamentary Reports, and after the troubles in the North, I hoped somebody like... you would be fighting for the Reforms which are so long overdue."

The Marquis looked at her in astonishment.

He knew she was referring to the uprising among the workers in Manchester which had resulted in a number of deaths and twelve thousand people being wounded.

When those who had rebelled against the misery and privation of their lot had been crushed and severely punished, it seemed as if all their efforts had been in vain.

At the same time, those who had declared in Parliament and elsewhere that Reforms were essential had increased their arguments against the Government, which had refused to listen to them.

"I am afraid politics does not interest me particularly," the Marquis remarked.

"But it should," Lucia objected. "I feel sure that the Prime Minister and the Cabinet would listen if . . . you fought against the many injustices which are being perpetrated all over the country."

The Marquis thought with a sense of amusement that she was talking to him exactly as Alastair had, and he said:

"I cannot think why people will not leave me alone! I am perfectly content with my successes in sporting circles, with the management of my houses and Estates, and with entertaining my friends."

There was silence, and he knew that Lucia did not agree with him.

Somewhat aggressively he asked:

"All right, say aloud what you are thinking—that what I do is wrong!"

"I am sure you would never do anything wrong," Lucia replied softly, "but when somebody is as dynamic and intelligent . . . as you are . . . your country needs you in time of peace just as your . . . leadership was essential in . . . war."

The Marquis sat back in his chair and looked at her as though he could hardly believe she was real.

He had never before dined with a beautiful woman who had taken him to task for not doing more in the national interest.

Usually on such occasions the conversation revolved

104

round what they would do together, and as far as she was concerned, the country did not exist.

"Are you really suggesting that I should proclaim from a soap-box, like the agitators in Hyde Park, the whining and grumbling of a small minority who cannot get themselves heard otherwise?" he asked for the sake of argument.

"Are you quite sure it is a small minority?" Lucia replied. "From all I read before I left England and the little I have been able to read in Venice, it appears that a very great number of people are most dissatisfied, however complacent the great landlords and those who sit in the House of Lords may be."

If the Marquis had been attacked by one of the birds that flew round them in the harbour, he could not have been more astonished.

To him it seemed incredible that anybody as ethereal and feminine should speak to him in the same way that one of his contemporaries might have done.

"I know exactly what you are saying, Lucia," he said. "I will be frank and say that there are plenty of people to worry themselves over the down-trodden poor, the democratic rights of the Catholics, and wrangling over the pocket-Boroughs. I, myself, am not particularly interested."

"But you must be," Lucia said earnestly. "Can you not see that those people have so few spokesmen with your brains and with your influence? That is why only somebody like . . . you can help them."

The Marquis felt that ordinarily he would have laughed such a suggestion to scorn.

Yet, there was something persuasive about the way Lucia spoke, and perhaps it was because he was in Venice and was still affected by the events of the day that he found himself almost hypnotised into believing that he was neglecting his duty.

"Why should I become the champion of the under-dog?" he asked with a slightly aggressive note in his voice.

"The answer to that is quite simple," Lucia replied. "Because you are an 'upper-dog'!"

The Marquis laughed as if he could not help it.

"I see you have an answer to everything, but when I arrive back in England I have so many things waiting for me to do that I doubt if I shall have time even to think about anything else."

"But you will try . . . please promise me you will . . . try."

The word "promise" made him think of how Francesca had said that Englishmen always kept their promises and he had replied to her that he always kept his.

He had a feeling that Lucia was manoeuvring him into a corner from which it would be difficult for him to extricate himself.

"If I once become a fanatic on the subject of reform, like Corbett and Wilberforce," he said, "you would undoubtedly find me a crashing bore."

Lucia laughed, and it was a very pretty sound.

"That is something you could never be," she said. "But the more I read about what is happening in England today, the more I feel worried and distressed that not enough great people like yourself are deeply concerned."

"How do you know I am a 'great person' in that sort of way?" the Marquis enquired.

Lucia made a little gesture with her hands that was very expressive.

"It is . . . difficult to put into words," she said, "but . . . I know the sun will rise tomorrow, and the sea will not . . . drain away during the night."

"I certainly hope not!"

Lucia was not listening.

She had put her elbow on the table, her hand on her cheek.

"Papa said once that we all transmit the life force, but some people transmit more than others, and they become great, like Buddha or Christ or Mohammed, or, in a lesser way, Marco Polo and Christopher Columbus."

"And you think I qualify to be in such distinguished company?" the Marquis asked mockingly.

There was a little silence. Then Lucia said in a low voice:

"I knew . . . as soon as I saw you . . . that you were . . . different. Then when I spoke to you in the Piazza San Marco I knew that you 'vibrated,' as Papa would say . . . very differently from . . . anybody else I had ever met."

"I am very flattered," the Marquis said drily, "but I think perhaps you are prejudiced."

"Perhaps I am, but at the same time you know I am speaking the truth."

The Marquis held up his hands in mock surrender.

"Now you are frightening me," he said, "and since you are also pressurising me into doing what I do not wish to do, it makes me determined to resist you."

Lucia shook her head.

"You may think you will do that, but I am quite certain, because you are you, that sooner or later you will know what has to be done, and you will do it!"

"If you continue to nag me," the Marquis replied, "I think before this voyage is over I shall throw you overboard and leave you to drown!"

As he spoke, he felt he was twisting and evading what Lucia was suggesting as if he had been caught like a fish on a hook.

It made him remember how he had told Alastair that that was how he felt when he avoided matrimony, but he had a feeling that this was even more constraining, and he said:

"I would like to point out to you, Lucia, that when you dine alone with a man you should amuse him, make him laugh, and not force him to think about himself when he should be thinking about you."

He saw the colour come into her cheeks before she said in a low voice:

"I . . . I am sorry . . . Mama always told me a man was . . . bored if a woman talked . . . too much."

Because he felt he had been unkind, the Marquis put out his hand.

"I am not in the least bored," he said. "I am only afraid that I shall be converted by a very able Missionary before I reach England."

He laid his hand invitingly on the table and Lucia put her fingers on his palm.

"I will try to . . . amuse you," she said, "but as you are no doubt aware, I am very . . . ignorant."

"Not intellectually."

"Then ignorant of how to amuse a very sophisticated gentleman."

His fingers closed over hers.

"Now you are being deliberately provocative," he said, "but let me tell you, Lucia, I have enjoyed our dinner together and I expect to enjoy a great many more."

He spoke seriously, and yet unaccountably she blushed again, and the Marquis released her hand.

"Now you must go to bed," he said. "You have been through a great deal today, and I know you will not admit it, but you are tired. Run along, child, and leave me to my thoughts, which are not at all what I expected to have tonight."

Somewhat uncertainly, because he was talking in quite a different manner from how he had before, Lucia rose from the table.

She stood beside his chair, looking at him for a moment. Then she said:

"Thank you for being so kind to me . . . and for arranging . . . Papa's Funeral. I shall . . . never forget what you have done . . . and I can only thank you . . . in my prayers."

As she finished speaking she bent forward and pressed her lips for a moment against the Marquis's hand, which still lay on the table.

Before he could speak or move, she had left the Saloon and he heard her footsteps running away towards her cabin.

The Marquis listened until there was silence.

Then he sat at the table thinking for a long time, until

the candles began guttering low and the stars had come out in the sky above.

* * *

In her cabin, Lucia stood for a moment with her hands against her cheeks.

She could not make up her mind whether she was blushing because she had made so many mistakes, or if it was because the Marquis's voice had been kind when he had sent her to bed and said he had really enjoyed being with her.

'He is so magnificent,' she thought, 'and he should be marching to victory or ruling as King over a country where there is no injustice, no starvation, and no cruelty.'

As she thought about him and all that he had done for her, she felt as if he grew larger and larger until he filled the whole sky, and there was nothing else but him.

She went to the port-hole to pull back the curtains and look out into the night.

"Perhaps he is right and I should try to amuse him and make him laugh," she told herself.

Then she felt as if, despite the manner in which he had argued with her, he had in fact responded to what she had said in some way which she could not put into words.

"He *did* understand," she told herself. "He *did* know it was what he should do."

She thought of the years when she and her mother had pored over the Reports in Parliament and the articles in the newspapers revealing the miseries of the workmen and the protests which had erupted at Peterloo—all asking for Reforms that should long ago have been initiated by Parliament.

Yet, even in Little Morden they had been aware of the apathy of the Government after the war, and of the terrible sufferings of the men who had been crippled and disbanded without pensions or any recompense for the sacrifices they had made while fighting for their country.

Apart from all these, there was always the horror of slavery, the suffering of the "climbing boys" who cleaned the chimneys, the iniquities of the "Flesh Houses" which were allowed to exist in London and other large Cities, and the cruelty of children slaving in the coal-mines.

Because Lucia was very sensitive, she found it incredible that all these things should be taking place while the wealthy aristocrats were gambling, racing their horses, and, like the King, running up a mountain of debts.

She had always been certain from the time she had seen him at the Steeple-Chase that the Marquis was different.

Although his name seldom figured in the debates in the House of Lords, she had somehow thought that he would fight against all the injustices that she and her mother found so distressing.

When he had come to her assistance, when he had been so understanding about her father's paintings and so unbelievably kind to her, she had thought it impossible for him to be anything that was not great and noble.

But today there had been first Francesca, and now when he had said at dinner that he was not interested in politics, she had felt almost as if he had dealt her a blow.

He was not what she had thought him to be, and yet she was well aware that as a man he still had that strange, irresistible vibration which she had never found in any other person she had met except her father.

In the Marquis it was unmistakable and inescapable, and she knew as she started to undress that although it seemed very presumptuous, she must, before the end of the voyage, make him believe in himself and his destiny.

Chapter Six

The Marquis and Lucia went on deck after they had finished dinner.

The sea had been rough for the first few days while they were in the Adriatic, then after they had passed Brindisi and sailed round the heel of Italy into the Mediterranean, the sea was as blue and almost as calm as the lagoon.

Because there was always the fear of pirates if they were anywhere near the north coast of Africa, the Marquis had given instructions that they should sail through the Strait of Messina between Italy and Sicily and up the west coast of Italy.

Now, looking out, they could see lights in the distance which seemed to mingle with the stars coming out in the sky overhead.

"It is so beautiful!" Lucia said after a moment.

There was silence. Then the Marquis said in a different voice from any she had heard before:

"So are you, Lucia!"

As she looked up in astonishment, he put his arms round her and drew her close to him.

Then, while she trembled because she thought she was stepping into a dream, his lips came down on hers.

She could hardly believe it was happening.

Yet, as the Marquis kissed her, she knew it was what she had been longing for not only in the days since they had been at sea in his yacht, but almost from the first moment she had known him.

But because he had seemed as far out of reach as the moon, or like a super-human being who had come from the Heavens to assist her, she had never imagined that he would touch her or hold her captive as he was doing now.

Because it was exactly as she had thought a kiss should be, she surrendered herself to his lips, feeling at the same time an ecstasy that was different from anything she had ever known before.

It was part of the light in which her father believed, the beauty of Venice, the glory of music, and flowers.

They were all there in a strange, mystical rapture that carried her away into the sky so that she was no longer on earth but part of the Divine.

As if he knew what she was feeling, and the softness and innocence of her mouth excited him, the Marquis's arms tightened, and his lips became more demanding, more insistent, more possessive.

There was a strange fire in them that made Lucia feel as if a warm wave moved through her body.

It became more and more intense in her breasts and in her throat until finally when it reached her lips she was joined to the Marquis with a burning flame that was, in itself, a rapture.

Only when a century seemed to have passed and the Marquis raised his head did she say in a voice that was barely above a whisper:

"I . . . I . . . love you! And I did not . . . know that a kiss could be . . . like that."

"I have been wanting to kiss you for a long time," the Marquis said in a deep voice, "but I was afraid to frighten you."

"I am . . . not frightened," Lucia answered. "I feel as if you have given me something so . . . magical . . . so perfect that there are . . . no words in which I can tell you how . . . wonderful it was."

The Marquis did not answer, but merely kissed her

again, and to Lucia it was as if they were both standing in a dazzling light which came not from the sky but from within themselves.

'Light is . . . love,' she thought.

Then there was nothing else in the whole world but the Marquis, his arms, his lips, and him.

* * *

Later, when it seemed as if the feelings they had evoked in each other were too intense to be borne, Lucia put her head on the Marquis's shoulder, and he knew her breath was coming quickly from between her lips.

"Could anyone be more adorable or more entrancing?" he asked. "And you are so different from anyone I have ever known before."

"Is that . . . true?"

"I will swear it to you, if you like. I have never known a kiss that was so wonderful or felt for any woman what I feel for you."

Lucia drew in her breath.

"I never . . . thought, I never . . . imagined that you would . . . kiss me."

"I know that," the Marquis smiled, "but every night when you have been arguing with me, and trying to convince me that I must become a crusader, I have been wanting to talk to you far more intimately."

"Did I . . . bore you?" she asked quickly.

"How could you bore me?" he replied. "I can assure you of one thing, my darling, no-one has ever been bored when they are in love."

He felt her quiver and she said:

"I . . . cannot believe it . . . I cannot believe that you . . . love me . . . but I suppose it was . . . inevitable that I . . . should fall in love with you . . . although I think actually I was . . . worshipping you."

"You are making me conceited—at the same time very proud. All I can promise you, my precious, is that I will look after you, and never again will you be alone or afraid."

Lucia gave a sigh that seemed to come from the very depths of her being.

"That is what I want you to say. I was so . . . dreading what would happen when we . . . arrived in England . . . and I was wishing that *The Sea Horse* would go very . . . very slowly."

"We will make plans," the Marquis said, "but for the moment I want only to kiss you."

His lips were on hers again, and he kissed her until she was trembling with the wonder of it, and felt that he was trembling too.

Then he said:

"How could I know there was anybody like you in the world? And yet I suppose from the first moment I saw you standing beside me in the *Piazza* outside Florian's, I should have realised, because I was so conscious of you, that I would never be able to escape."

"Do you . . . want to?"

"You are well aware that is a very foolish question," he replied. "We are one person, Lucia; we know what the other is thinking, and we vibrate towards each other, so that you are mine now and forever."

"That is . . . what I want . . . to be."

"That is what you are, and I will say it again and again until you believe me, for if I cannot escape, neither can you."

As he spoke he moved his lips softly over her forehead and down her straight little nose, and when her mouth was ready for his kiss, instead he kissed her small, pointed chin.

His lips gave her a strange feeling, then unexpectedly the Marquis bent lower and kissed the softness of her neck.

It was then that Lucia felt as if shafts of starlight were streaking through her body.

They gave her a sensation that was half-ecstasy, half-pain, so that her breath came in little gasps and her body moved against the Marquis's.

"My sweet! My darling!" he exclaimed.

Then his lips were on hers, kissing her passionately and possessively in a way he had not done before.

Lucia knew he was right when he had said that they were one person, and she melted into him and no longer had any identity of her own.

Only when she felt that no-one could experience such rapture and still be alive did the Marquis ask:

"Why should we wait? I want you now, at this moment, but I want to tell you first of my plans."

Because Lucia was feeling dazed and bewildered with the emotions he had evoked in her, she found it impossible to reply and once again put her head against his shoulder.

"You mentioned your old Nanny," the Marquis said as if he was forcing himself to speak sensibly, "but I thought that instead of your going to her as you decided to do, you could bring her to London."

Lucia was puzzled but she did not speak, and he continued:

"She can look after you in a house that I will buy for you as near as possible to mine so that there will be no question of your being alone, and I will be with you every moment that I can."

It was difficult for Lucia to think of anything but the light that seemed to come from the Marquis and herself.

It blinded not only her eyes but her mind, and once again she merely gave a little murmur, finding it difficult to understand what he was saying.

"We will be very, very happy," the Marquis went on. "I promise—and you know I never break my promises—that if a hundred years from now we have to part from each other, I will provide for you and you will never want for anything or be poor as you were in Venice."

It was then, as if trying to grasp what he was saying, that Lucia came out of her trance.

"I . . . I do not . . . understand."

"There is plenty of time to talk about it later," the

115

Marquis said, "but now, my lovely one, I only want to kiss you and teach you about love."

His lips were very near to hers as he said:

"As I said just now, why should we wait? We love each other, and you are mine, mine, my precious, forever!"

Before she could reply, before she could ask him what he was saying, he was kissing her again.

Now the fire on his lips seemed to burn its way into her whole body, and she felt as if there were flames leaping in her breast which grew in intensity with every kiss the Marquis gave her.

Then, so suddenly that she almost fell, he took his arms from her to say:

"I cannot wait any longer! Go down to your cabin, my sweet, and I will join you in a few minutes."

Then, as if his words shattered her dream, and the light that dazzled her was dimmed and she saw more clearly, she said:

"What ... are you ... saying? What are you ... asking me ... to do?"

"I am telling you that I love you," the Marquis replied, "and the most thrilling thing I have ever done in my life will be to teach you about love."

He put his arms round her again as he said:

"I will be very gentle, and will not frighten you, but I want you and I will make you want me."

His voice was deep and hoarse with passion, but it seemed to Lucia as if the fire flickering within her suddenly died down, almost as if blown out by a cold wind.

She put both her hands on the Marquis's chest, forcing him a little way away from her. Then she said in a voice that did not seem like her own:

"What ... are you ... asking me to ... do?"

"I am asking you to love me, my darling, as I love you!"

"I do ... love you ... I love you with all my heart ... but there is still ... something I do not ... understand."

The Marquis was smiling as he said:

"There is more to loving than kisses, and that is why I want you close to me, and to explain how wonderful love can be when two people feel as we do."

Again Lucia felt as if a cold wind swept through her, and her body was stiff and unyielding as she said in a voice he could barely hear:

"Are you . . . asking me to be your . . . mistress?"

As she spoke she could see Francesca's eyes flashing in her beautiful face, and hear the raw passion in her voice as she raised the stiletto to strike at the Marquis.

At her question the Marquis stiffened too. Then he said:

"My precious, I do not want you to think of it like that."

"But . . . that is . . . what you are . . . asking."

"Words are not important, names do not matter. What we are talking about is us—you and me, Lucia."

"What you are . . . suggesting is . . . wrong."

"Who is to decide that?" the Marquis asked. "My darling, be practical. What alternative is there for you except to try to earn your living, which I am sure you are quite incapable of doing, alone and unprotected."

Lucia did not speak, and after a moment the Marquis went on:

"I promise that I will look after you. We shall be very happy together, and while we are in London I will come to the house which I am giving you with your old Nanny. But there will be many times when we can be together in *The Sea Horse* or visit France and anywhere else in the world."

He spoke beguilingly, as if he was tempting her, but while his arms were still round her, Lucia felt as if there were a great gulf between them.

Then, almost as if she was seeing a picture in front of her eyes, she remembered the expression on the Marquis's face as he had looked at Francesca, and heard again the cold, icy anger in his voice as he had told her to leave.

It was then that she knew that she could not explain, could not argue, but she could not stay with him.

With a little cry like that of a small animal that had been hurt, she said:

"No! No . . . no!"

Before the Marquis could stop her, she had run away from him, leaving the deck and disappearing below to her cabin.

He took a step as if he would follow her.

Then he turned to hold on to the rail and look out at the lights on the land and the stars overhead without seeing them.

* * *

In her cabin, Lucia locked the door and flung herself down on her bed, hiding her face in her pillow.

She was trembling so convulsively that for the moment she felt almost as if her teeth were chattering.

Then as she tried to think, she felt that her brain had ceased to function, and it was hard to breathe.

She lay feeling as if she had dropped down into a dark dungeon and she could not find the way out.

It was quite a long time before she could think clearly, and then she asked herself over and over again:

"How could he . . . expect me to . . . do such a . . . thing? How could he . . . imagine I was that . . . sort of woman?"

She remembered the men who had followed her in Venice. They had thought she was "that sort of woman," and that they should have thought in such a way was degrading and humiliating.

But for the Marquis, of all people, to expect her to take the place of Francesca, whom he had just discarded, and to suggest that he should give her a house in payment for their love, was to make her feel as if she were drowning in a pool of filth and slime.

"How could he? How could he dare even to think that I would agree to such a suggestion?" she asked herself.

The same question repeated and repeated itself for a long time.

Then gradually as she became calmer and ceased to tremble, she found herself striving to think logically.

But that was impossible, because the moment she thought of the Marquis as a man, all she could remember was the wonder and the glory of his kisses and the sensations he had aroused in her when he kissed her neck.

"I love him! I love him!" she said into the darkness.

Now because of her love the tears choked her and began to run down her cheeks.

Fearing she might sob out loud and the Marquis would hear her, she turned her face into the pillow and cried until she was almost suffocating.

In fact, it was an hour before she rose from the bed, took off her evening-dress and put on her nightgown, and slid between the sheets.

She did not know whether the Marquis had gone to bed or even if he had come to her door perhaps to apologise or to plead with her.

She knew only that her tears had been so tempestuous that while she cried she had been unconscious of anything else.

She felt utterly exhausted. At the same time, her mind seemed to have cleared, and she could think, as she had been unable to do before.

Now lying in bed, she went over exactly what had happened, and for the first time was aware that in a foolish, child-like way she had always imagined that if she loved a man and he loved her, they would be married.

She was well aware that it would be impossible for the Marquis to marry anybody like her.

Her mother had told her of the importance and the responsibilities of the aristocratic Englishmen.

"They are almost like Kings of their own Estates, darling," she had said with a smile. "Their people look to them for guidance and protection, and to all intents and purposes their word is law!"

She had then explained to Lucia that noble families married into other noble families and a *mesalliance* was always frowned on.

"It is only in fairy-stories and novelettes," she had

said, "that the 'goose-girl' can marry the Prince, and I am sure you realise it is something which does not happen in the real world."

"But sometimes, Mama, the Princess marries the swine-herd," Lucia had remarked.

Her mother had laughed, then went on to say:

"All that really matters, my darling, is that two people when they marry should love each other. Nothing else, and I mean nothing else, is of any importance."

Now Lucia knew that that was not the answer to her problem.

She had never for one moment imagined that the Marquis would ask her to marry him, and she knew from what he had said that he had never thought of marrying her.

Of course, if she was practical, the only position she could occupy in his life was that of his mistress, and if she was sensible, it was a position she should accept because she had no alternative.

Then she thought that to do so would destroy the ideals and the appreciation of beauty with which she had been brought up ever since she was a baby.

It was beauty which had counted in the small cottage in which they had lived in Little Morden.

It was beauty which her mother had given to her father and her, and it was beauty which her father had sought to portray in his paintings.

The beauty of life and of love, and the two were synonymous.

"It would be wicked of me to destroy that," Lucia argued with herself, "not only because the Church would call it a sin, but because it would be a sin against my soul and everything in which I believe."

It was then that she found herself questioning whether or not her mother had been right when she said love was more important than anything else.

She remembered the rapture the Marquis had aroused

in her and the wonder of his lips, until once again the tears began to run down her cheeks.

"I love . . . him! I love . . . him!" she sobbed.

Then she knew that whatever he asked her to do and however humiliating she might find it, she still loved him to the exclusion of everything else.

* * *

The Marquis stood for a long time on the deck.

He did not realise that the ship was moving towards the shore until he was aware that the lights had grown nearer and he knew that the Captain was making for a quiet harbour in which they could spend the night.

He always found it better for the crew and for his own comfort, if it was possible, to drop anchor from about midnight to dawn, then set off fresh in the morning.

As Captain Bateson knew the coast well, the Marquis had left the choice of stopping-places to him.

Now as the yacht drew nearer and there were few lights, he was sure that they were about to enter a quiet bay in which there would be no curious people to stare at them, and they would be able to pass the night completely undisturbed.

Then his thoughts were once again on Lucia, and he was wondering what he could do about her.

He had to some extent anticipated that she might be shocked at his suggestion that he should become her protector.

Yet, he asked himself, what else could he do but offer to look after her, save her from being alone and, he was certain, menaced by other men?

As Lucia had known, the Marquis had a very clear idea of his own consequence and was extremely proud of his heritage.

He had told Alastair that he had no intention of marrying, but at the same time he was aware that sooner or later he must have an heir, and that meant he would have to acquire a wife.

121

However, there was no hurry, and he had no intention of marrying until it was absolutely imperative for him to do so.

He knew, as he had known ever since he was a small boy, that his wife must be his equal in her position in Society, for any woman who bore his name had a traditional part to play not only in the County where his family had lived for five generations but also at Court.

As well as it being obligatory for his wife to be the Patron of many Charities, Orphanages, Schools, and Hospitals, as his mother had been, the Marchioness of Wynchcombe was traditionally Lady-of-the-Bedchamber to the Queen when there was one.

The Marquis, while dreading the moment when he would be married, was well aware that to make a *mesalliance*, as the King had done in choosing the wrong consort, could be disastrous, not only from his point of view but also from his family's.

Therefore, he had never for one moment envisaged that he would find the woman who was suitable to be his wife anywhere but in the Drawing-Rooms of Mayfair or the Ball-Room at Buckingham Palace.

Now, insidiously, almost as if the Devil himself were putting the idea into his mind, he found himself thinking that if he had to be married, and God knew he had no wish to be, then he would be happy only with Lucia.

"I not only want her physically," he told himself, "but she stimulates my mind and makes me think in a manner in which I have not done since I was at Oxford."

He remembered that in those days he had had a chivalrous idea of women, and that he and his friends would sit talking into the night of the ideals which had made the Knights of Malta take the vow of chastity.

Because they themselves wished to reform the world, they had discussed whether they should do likewise.

It was half serious, half play-acting, and yet now the Marquis thought that that was a time in his life when he had really believed himself to be a crusader for everything that was highest and best in the enlightenment of mankind.

Then, when he had left Oxford to join the Army, there had been women, and more women, to make him forget anything but the exotic and sensual pleasures of the body.

When he went to war he had found it hard to think of anything but the necessity of keeping alive.

After that, he had returned to England to be a leader in the wild and raffish *Beau Monde*.

As one of the closest friends of the Regent, he was expected to enjoy the company of women and all the other pleasures of the flesh.

"Dammit all, that is what I still want!" the Marquis said sharply to himself.

Then all he could see was the light in Beaumont's paintings and the spiritual beauty of Lucia's face.

He was aware how much Francesca must have startled and shocked her, following on top of the emotions she had felt when her father was buried.

Yet no-one, he knew, could have behaved more bravely or in a more dignified manner, and no-one could have been quicker and more intelligent in saving his life.

"I love her!" he admitted to himself in the darkness, just as Lucia was saying the same thing in the cabin next door.

"I love her! I love her!" the Marquis repeated beneath his breath.

Then he asked himself almost despairingly how, even if he wished to, he could marry the daughter of an artist.

It was no use pretending even for a moment that artists, however famous, however acclaimed, were accepted in the Social World as the equals of those who commissioned and paid for their paintings.

Artists were tradesmen—superior tradesmen, it was true, but still tradesmen—who accepted money in return for their wares.

The Marquis remembered that his father would never have thought of inviting any of the artists who came to his house to sit down with him to a meal.

They came to advise him on his paintings, or to bring him new ones to add to his famous collection, but if they ate they did so in a room by themselves, and certainly not with their Patron.

As the Marquis tossed and turned in his bed, he found himself wanting Lucia with an intensity that made him want to break down her door and force himself upon her.

"If I make her mine," he thought, "then there will be no more arguments in the future and she must rely on me because she has no alternative."

Then he knew that even if physically he could overcome her resistance, he could not violate her spirit.

No other woman had made him feel so protective that he had known from the first moment he saw her. that he would have to save her from everything that filled her eyes with fear.

He had fought against this, telling himself it was just an illusion, and yet when her father died and Lucia turned to him for comfort, he had known there was no escape, and she was his.

"What can I do? What the devil can I do?" the Marquis asked.

It was only when the first faint glow on the horizon heralded the dawn that he knew the answer.

* * *

Lucia also had been unable to sleep.

After a little while she gave up praying that she might do so, and sat up against the pillows.

It was very quiet except for the soft lap of the waves against the sides of the yacht, and as she had not drawn the curtains over the port-holes, she could see the stars in the sky outside.

She remembered how the Marquis had quoted John Donne to her and said he wished to "catch a falling star."

"That is what I want to help him to do," she told herself miserably.

Once again she was remembering how she had told him how much there was for him to do in the House of Lords and in the country.

'He is so intelligent and has so much presence,' she thought, 'that he could make people listen to him, and although he tries not to admit it, the Reforms we spoke of are very necessary. I know I could help him to understand what needs to be done.'

Suddenly, as if her mother were talking to her as they had talked so often in the past, she found herself planning what she would say to the Marquis and the arguments she would present to him almost in the form of a plea which he would not be able to refuse.

Then as the stars began to fade and the first glow of the dawn appeared on the horizon, she knew that it was love that counted more than anything else.

Because she loved the Marquis, and because the good he could do in the world was more important even than her principles and her conscience, she must do what he asked.

"Perhaps I shall be . . . punished for it, Mama," she said in a low voice, as if her mother were listening, "and perhaps eventually he will . . . turn me away, as he did the Venetian woman, with . . . hatred in his heart and his eyes like steel, but at least by that time I will have made him . . . aware of how important he is and what he is capable of doing."

She waited, as if her mother would reply, and when she did not do so she said:

"You loved Papa so overwhelmingly, and it was entirely due to the happiness you gave him that he painted so brilliantly."

She paused as she thought of her father's paintings and how year by year his skill had increased in transferring the light of life which he felt within himself onto the canvass in front of him.

But it was her mother who had encouraged and inspired her father and made him aware that even if no-one understood or appreciated his paintings, it was still his duty to paint them for the future.

"One day somebody will understand," she had said, "and, darling, that is the gift you are giving to the world."

"I am sure, Mama," Lucia went on, "that just as you made Papa realise he must never give up and that the light in his paintings came from God, so I can give the Marquis the same light to lead those who need his leadership to understand what compassion, understanding, and justice demand."

The first gleam of the sun rose in the sky, and as it did so it came through the cabin in a faint diffusion of light that seemed to Lucia the answer for which she had been seeking.

It was as if her mother were speaking to her and telling her that the love she had for the Marquis was a gift from God and must not be wasted.

"I will tell him that I will do what he . . . wants, and pray that he will not too . . . quickly find me boring and send me . . . away from him," Lucia decided.

She was not certain exactly what being the mistress of a man entailed, but she was sure that if the Marquis made love to her, it would be as wonderful and as perfect as his kisses had been.

He had said he felt differently about her and loved her as he had never loved any other woman, so she wanted to believe that there would be no comparison in his loving between herself and Francesca, or any of the other women in his life.

And yet she knew that because of the way she had been brought up to believe that love was a part of God, she would always feel that what she was doing was a sin, even though she must never say so.

"I will pray and pray to be forgiven," she told herself, "and perhaps because I shall be helping the Marquis to help other people, I will not feel so . . . ashamed and degraded."

But however much she argued with herself, she could still see Francesca's painted face and sensational appearance.

That had proclaimed, Lucia thought, not only her theatrical profession but also that she was like the women who were escorted by the aristocrats of Venice.

Her mother had looked at them scornfully and refused to discuss them.

"There are women no lady notices, dearest," she had said to Lucia.

"They are very flamboyant, Mama," Lucia had said once when they were attending the Opera.

She had seen them waving from one Box to another, laughing uproariously and flirting outrageously with their gentlemen-friends.

"Watch the stage, Lucia!" her mother had said sharply. "And remember that to a lady, such creatures do not even exist."

But they did exist, Lucia thought now, and the Marquis had asked her to become one of them.

She wondered if he would want her to paint her face and if he would give her jewels as he had given them to Francesca.

When she was with him, ladies like her mother would look through her, and for them she would not exist.

She felt herself shudder in the same way as she had shuddered and shrunk from the men who had pursued her in Venice.

Then she knew that if the Marquis was not beside her and she was alone, there would be men to menace her wherever she went.

Even if she buried herself in Little Morden and saw only Nanny and the villagers for the rest of her life, they would still find her.

"What else can I do?" she asked herself. "When the

money the Marquis will pay me for the paintings is finished, I shall have to earn my living somehow."

Just as if her thoughts had gone round in a circle, she was back where she started, knowing that however reprehensible it was, she would be safe with the Marquis.

Then she need not be afraid of anything except for the moment when he would no longer need her, and she also would be working to inspire him to "catch a falling star."

"I will do it," she decided again, "but... please, God... help me."

* * *

The sun became more golden as it rose above the horizon, and there was the sound of footsteps on the deck overhead.

Lucia got up and dressed herself, finding that because the tumult of the night was past and her mind was made up, she felt quite calm.

She felt, because she had lived through a Gethsemane of her own, that it should have left some mark on her face.

Instead, as the sunshine came into the cabin it lit her eyes, found the gold of her hair, and illuminated the clearness of her skin.

'It is because, despite everything, I love him!' she thought.

As she put on one of her simple gowns which was limp with so many washes, she could feel her heart beating tumultuously because in a few minutes she would see the Marquis again.

She thought how glad he would be that she was prepared to be amenable.

He would smile at her, and perhaps he would kiss her again, so that she would find it impossible to think of anything but the rapture he aroused in her and that she loved him beyond life itself.

That was the truth.

And finally, when he no longer wanted her in his life, then it would be quite easy to die.

"I shall live and love, for without him I shall feel as

Papa felt when Mama died, that there was nothing more to live for," she told herself.

She took a last glance in the mirror and thought that she had arranged her chair in a particularly becoming way, and that her eyes were shining—or was it just the sun coming through the port-hole?

Then as she looked at her mouth and remembered the Marquis's kisses of the night before, she blushed.

She was almost sure her lips now looked different because it was through them that he had given her such ecstasy that it had carried her away from the earth and into the sky.

'I love him!' she thought, and knew that all she wanted was to be with him again, and for him to reassure her that despite the way she had behaved last night, he still loved her and wanted her.

Then, almost like the feeling of a cold hand on her heart, she wondered if perhaps because she had run away he had changed his mind and would no longer offer her a little house in London near his, with Nanny to look after her, but instead would prefer somebody like Francesca.

Then she told herself that she was being needlessly apprehensive.

The love they had both felt could not vanish overnight, but came from eternity and would go on to eternity.

Then, as if she needed desperately to be reassured, she ran across her cabin to open the door.

As she did so, the door of the Master Suite opened at the same time and the Marquis was there.

For a moment they both stood still, and as their eyes met, it was as if they were both turned to stone.

Then, trembling and finding it difficult to find her voice, Lucia began:

"I . . . I have . . . something to tell . . ."

The Marquis moved forward and took her hand in his.

"Forgive me, my darling," he said in his deep voice, "and tell me how soon you will marry me."

Chapter Seven

*L*ucia was stunned into silence, and while she tried to find her voice she could only stare at the Marquis.

Then he said with a smile:

"I am going for a walk. As we have a lot to say to each other, will you come with me?"

He put out his hand as he spoke, and as she put hers into it, she felt again as if his vibrations joined hers and they were one person.

Just as she was, she went with him up on deck.

There she saw that he had obviously given his orders, for a boat was waiting to row them the short distance to the shore.

The ship was anchored in a very attractive bay with a low cliff at the far end of it, and Lucia found when she reached it that it had well-cut steps in the rock which made it easy to climb.

First she had to clamber down a rope-ladder into the boat, and the Marquis went first so as to help her.

When his hands touched her waist, she felt a little tremor go through her and was sure he was aware of it.

The sailors rowed them to the centre of the bay where there was a small jetty from which they could step ashore.

"Come back in an hour," the Marquis told them, then followed Lucia along the jetty and onto the beach.

Without speaking, they climbed the steps and found

at the top of them there was some rough ground on which small shrubs were growing heavy with blossom.

Beyond was a line of mimosa trees as golden as the sun and as beautiful as the early-morning light that was just filling the sky.

The Marquis again took Lucia's hand in his, and they walked for a little way through the trees until they came to a seat looking out towards the sea.

They were obviously in a beauty spot which later in the year could be enjoyed by summer visitors.

At the moment it was too early for there to be anybody in sight, and as the Marquis paused by the seat, Lucia sat down and raised her eyes to his.

He sat beside her. Then, taking both her hands in his, he said:

"I love you! I lay awake last night thinking of how I had hurt you, and I realised that nothing in the world is more important than our love."

As that was exactly what Lucia had thought, her fingers tightened on his and she murmured:

"I was . . . thinking of . . . you too."

"I was sure of it."

"I . . . I have . . . something to . . . say to you."

He smiled before he answered:

"I am listening. Do not take too long, my darling, for I want more than anything else to kiss you."

"No . . . please . . ." Lucia said, "you must first . . . hear what I . . . have to say."

She took her hand from his because it was difficult to talk when he was touching her, which made her think of nothing but the nearness of him and the feelings he aroused in her.

As if he understood, he leant back against the seat and put his arm along the back of it so that he could face her.

As she hesitated for words, he said:

"Could anybody be more lovely? Your face has haunted me, my precious, ever since I first saw you, and as far as I am concerned, no other woman exists in the whole world."

Because what he was saying moved her, he saw a tremor go through her, and he asked:

"What do you want to tell me?"

Clasping her hands together, Lucia answered:

"I . . . too was thinking last night of how . . . much I love you . . . and because I love you . . . I will . . . do what you . . . want."

"That is what I thought you might say, my darling," the Marquis answered, "but what I want is that you should be with me always and at all times, not just secretly or hidden away."

Lucia drew in her breath at the way he spoke. Then she said:

"That is . . . what I want too . . . but because it is impossible for . . . you to marry me . . ."

"I intend to marry you," the Marquis interrupted, "and it was only because I was being extremely stupid and very obtuse that last night I suggested anything different."

"No . . . no . . . you were . . . right," Lucia said. "We cannot lose our love . . . but at the same time I . . . cannot be your wife."

The Marquis smiled and it was very tender.

"You are thinking of me rather than of yourself, and I adore you for it, but I intend to marry you."

There was a little silence. Then Lucia said falteringly:

"I . . . I never imagined . . . never dreamt that you would ask me to be your . . . wife . . . because I knew it was impossible."

"Why should it be impossible?" the Marquis asked a little aggressively.

"You are so . . . important . . . and Mama explained to me that . . . aristocrats must marry aristocrats . . . and because of your position . . . you must be . . . proud of your wife."

"I shall always be very proud of you," the Marquis said quietly, "because of your beauty and your purity."

Lucia looked away from him and he thought her profile was so lovely and so perfect that it might have been that of a Greek goddess.

It flashed through his mind that nobody who looked at her would question for one moment that she was not as aristocratic as he was, with a pedigree to equal his.

Then Lucia turned to him again and said:

"I am honoured . . . deeply honoured that you should ask me to . . . marry you . . . but although I love you with all my heart, I cannot . . . be your wife."

Because she spoke so positively, the Marquis looked at her in astonishment before he said:

"Do you really think I would allow you to refuse me? I have made up my mind, Lucia, and nothing you can say, except that you no longer love me, will prevent us from being married!"

Lucia gave a little cry.

"Please . . . you must understand that . . . although I will love you forever and be with you for as . . . long as you want . . . me, there is no question of my being . . . able to marry you."

"Why not?"

The question came from the Marquis's lips like a pistol before he added:

"You cannot be—it is impossible that you are already married!"

"No . . . of course I am not married," Lucia said quickly, "but I cannot marry you . . . and there is no point in . . . saying any more."

The Marquis stared at her.

"Do you really think that I would accept that decision without your giving me a very good reason for it? You love me, Lucia, I know you love me as I love you! You must therefore explain in words I can understand why you would prefer to be my mistress rather than my wife."

He had deliberately intended to shock her by the way he spoke, and he saw the little shiver that went through her.

He knew she was thinking of Francesca and how much the Venetian's behaviour had appalled her.

Then he asked very quietly:

"What is this secret you are keeping from me? I think I have always known there has been something you are concealing."

"I . . . I do not think I should . . . tell you."

"It is something you have to do. Can you imagine that anybody, least of all the man who loves you, will allow you to hide something that would always stand between us as a barrier?"

Lucia did not speak, and after a moment he said:

"Whatever it is, whatever you have done, I will love you as I love you now and will still want you to be my wife."

The way he spoke made the tears come into Lucia's eyes, and after a moment she said:

"How can you be . . . so wonderful? How . . . can you always say the things I . . . want to hear? Things which speak to my . . . heart?"

"Just as you speak to mine," the Marquis said. "That is why, my beautiful one, there can be no secrets between us, now or in the future."

Again Lucia looked away from him, and he knew she was wondering what was the right thing to do.

"Whether you marry me, or whether we live together," he said quietly, "we are one person, Lucia, and nothing can part us except death, and I believe even then we will be together."

As if the words moved her more than she was already, the tears in her eyes overflowed and ran down her cheeks.

The Marquis made a little movement as if he would take her in his arms, then with an effort he prevented himself from doing so and merely said:

"Tell me, my darling, however difficult it may be, and I promise you that I will understand."

For a moment there was silence. Then Lucia said in a voice that did not seem like her own:

"I . . . I cannot marry you because I have . . . no real . . . identity. People would want to . . . know all about me as your wife . . . and if they should find out . . . it would . . . hurt you."

The Marquis looked puzzled. Then he said:

"I do not understand. Start from the beginning, my darling, and tell me about yourself."

"Mama said," Lucia answered, "that I was never to breathe a word to . . . anybody about it . . . except my husband."

Then quickly, in case the Marquis was too encouraged by what she said, she added:

"Mama never envisaged that I would marry anybody like you. In fact, she told me it was . . . impossible. She just hoped that I would love . . . an ordinary man to whom it would not . . . matter very much."

"As far as you are concerned, my precious little love," the Marquis answered, "I am the man who will be your husband, and nothing else is of the least importance."

Lucia put up her hand to wipe away the tears from her cheeks as she said with a faint smile:

"You know that is . . . not true. You cannot help being you . . . and that is what . . . makes it so difficult."

"Tell me your secret and I will decide how difficult it is," the Marquis said. "But I promise you, Lucia, before you go any further, there is nothing, no barrier, no difficulties, no crime that will keep us apart."

Lucia drew in her breath. Then she said almost in a whisper:

"Papa's . . . name was not . . . Beaumont, as you thought . . . but Beaufoy."

She felt the Marquis stiffen, but he did not speak, and she went on:

"He was in fact the . . . youngest son of the . . . Duke of Beauhampton!"

"Can this be true?"

Lucia nodded.

"But why? Why did he paint under an assumed name?"

"That is what I am about to tell you."

The Marquis leant forward to take her hand in his.

"I am listening, my darling."

"When my grandfather, the Duke, who is dead now... was over fifty," Lucia began, "he went to Europe during the Armistice with France to stay with an old friend, the Grand Duke Maximus of Valenstein."

As if she thought the Marquis did not understand, she said:

"Valenstein was a small country on the border of Austria, and I believe its people were very happy."

"I have heard of it," the Marquis said quietly.

"Before the Duke returned to England, he asked the Grand Duke if he could marry his youngest daughter... the Princess Ilena."

Lucia's voice altered as she said:

"The Princess, who was still in the School-Room, had hardly spoken to the Duke while he was staying in the Palace, and only after he had left was she told she was to marry him. Although she was astonished and perturbed, she knew there was nothing she could do about it."

"She did not wish to marry an Englishman?" the Marquis asked.

"It was not because he was English," Lucia said quickly, "because the Princess was in fact one-quarter English herself, her grandmother being English, and she had always longed to visit England."

There was a little pause before Lucia went on after a moment:

"But she had always dreamt of marrying somebody young and handsome, and although the Duke was a good-looking man, she felt he was very old."

"Go on," the Marquis prompted.

"I think you can guess what happened," Lucia answered. "The Princess was brought to England by her grandmother, to stay with the Duke on his Estate in Cornwall."

"How old was she?" the Marquis interposed.

"By the time the journey had been arranged, she was nearly eighteen, and although her grandmother the Dowager Duchess was very excited at the thought of the marriage, Princess Ilena felt very nervous."

Lucia's voice was very revealing as she continued:

"To marry a man who she learnt already had a grown-up family of three sons and two daughters was extremely frightening."

"I can understand that," the Marquis murmured.

"Then when the Princess arrived at the Duke's house in Cornwall," Lucia went on, "she met his youngest son, Bernard..."

"And they fell in love!"

"From the moment they saw each other, Mama said, it was as if Papa had a light blazing from him, and he felt the same way about her."

"What happened?"

"At first they thought despairingly that there was nothing they could do, and Papa decided to go abroad because he said he could not stay in the same country with Mama and see her married to his father."

"That is how I should have felt," the Marquis said.

"They were both very... unhappy, until Papa had an... idea."

"And what was that?"

"It was clever... but it needed very careful.... planning."

"What did they do?"

"First of all, Papa took his two best horses from the stables, and told the grooms he was selling them to a friend who lived not far away."

As if she felt the Marquis must understand every detail of what had happened, Lucia was speaking slowly and clearly as she said:

"Papa also smuggled out of the house all the clothes that he could carry on the back of his saddle and left them also at his friend's house."

She paused before she continued:

"It was more difficult for Mama, who had a lady's-maid with her, but she managed to give him one or two things that she felt were essential, and they too were conveyed secretly to Papa's friend."

Lucia gave a little sigh before she said:

"You can imagine how frightened they were, having made their plans, that they would be discovered at the last moment, or that the servants might be suspicious and tell either the Duke or my Mama's grandmother what was happening."

"It certainly must have been nerve-wracking," the Marquis agreed.

"Then, just four days before my mother, having seen her future home, was to return with the Duke to Valenstein for the wedding, she and Papa put their plan into operation."

"What did they do?"

"They left the house very early in the morning, and Mama left a note for her grandmother to say that Papa had promised to show her the dawn breaking over the Dragon Caves."

Lucia explained quickly:

"The Dragon Caves were very famous, and everybody who stayed with the Duke visited them, but one could only see them properly from a boat."

The Marquis was listening intently, and now he began to understand what had happened.

"Papa rowed Mama in a boat down the coast. Then he set her down on the shore, undressed, and having rowed the boat towards the cave, threw the oars overboard. Although he said it was a very difficult thing to do, he turned the boat over so that it was afloat upside-down."

"That was clever of him!" the Marquis exclaimed.

"Papa pushed the boat out to sea," Lucia continued, "before he swam back to the shore where he had left Mama. He put on his clothes and they hurried to a wood where his friend was waiting with the two horses."

The Marquis smiled.

"A very ingenious plan."

"They galloped away," Lucia went on, "putting as much distance between them and the Duke's house as they could before there was any likelihood of anyone worrying why they had not returned."

"And they got away with it?"

"The tragedy of their deaths was published in the newspapers, and it was also reported that it was expected that their bodies would be washed up on a different part of the coast."

Lucia gave a little laugh as she added:

"It was known how strong the currents were round the caves and that at times they could be dangerous."

"And nobody ever guessed they were alive?" the Marquis asked.

Lucia shook her head.

"Papa had some money of his own, and shortly before what was presumed to be his death he had drawn out all he had in the Bank, leaving a large overdraft."

"And that is what they had to live on?"

"They of course realised that they had to be very careful," Lucia said, "and when I was born two years later, in 1805, although they were thrilled to have me, I was an added expense."

"So they settled in Little Morden."

"Papa had visited Worchestershire when he was a young man and had thought it a quiet, isolated County. So they rode there, having, Mama said, a blissful honeymoon with nobody to disturb them, and found a tiny cottage they could rent for a few shillings a week."

Lucia's voice was very tender as she said:

"It was our . . . home and I . . . loved it very much."

"That I can understand," the Marquis said, "because your parents were two people who had dared everything for love."

"Of course they were always frightened that somebody would discover that they were not dead, for it would have caused a . . . great scandal."

"Of course it would," he agreed, "but they were not discovered."

"Mama encouraged Papa to paint because she realised how gifted he was, and, as I have already told you, when we grew very poor he was able to make some money by painting conventional pictures rather than the ones he preferred doing."

The Marquis did not speak, and after a moment she said:

"Now you... understand that because I really have no... name that I can use, and because... no-one must ever guess... who I am, I cannot marry anybody like you."

The Marquis put his arms round her and drew her close to him.

"Do you really think," he asked, "that as your father was so clever, we could not be as clever as he was, and not only avoid detection but make quite certain no-one sees any reason for being curious about you, as they would be if you were just 'Miss Beaumont from Nowhere'?"

Lucia looked up at him.

"What are you... saying? I do not... understand."

"I cannot allow you to underestimate my intelligence," the Marquis replied. "Your father and mother were clever enough all those years to escape detection, and we will do the same."

"It would be impossible... if I was your wife... for them not to ask questions," Lucia said quickly.

"I quite agree," the Marquis replied. "That is why we must have the right answers for them."

She looked at him in a puzzled way and asked:

"How can we do that?"

"I am just working it out," he said. "In the meantime, my precious, I want you to tell me again that nothing is important except our love, and that nothing will prevent you from loving me as I love you."

"I love you! I love you!" Lucia replied, "but..."

"There are no 'buts,'" the Marquis said, "because I

love you and I intend to marry you and we just have to be clever. But first of all, I am going to kiss you."

He put his fingers under her chin and lifted her face to his as he spoke.

Then he was kissing her with long, slow, passionate kisses which made her feel as if there were no problems, no difficulties, only a love which vibrated between them like the rising sun.

He kissed her until she felt the fire burning in her that had burnt the night before, and she knew his heart was beating as violently as hers.

Then he set her free.

"My precious, my darling," he said. "I intend to marry you at Nice, which is only two days' sailing away. I cannot wait any longer!"

"But I have just told you . . . we cannot be . . . married!"

"What you told me has made it very much easier, although you may not think so, than it was before."

"How can you say that?"

"Because, my adorable one," the Marquis said, "I am not going to marry 'Miss Beaumont' and have people questioning me as they undoubtedly will as to who your father and mother were! That would definitely be dangerous."

"Then what . . . can we do?"

The Marquis paused for a moment as if he was thinking it out. Then he said:

"I presume you know that Napoleon overran Valenstein at the time he fought the Austrians?"

"Yes, Mama knew that, and it upset her very much."

"What was left of the country," the Marquis went on, "was incorporated into the Austrian Empire, and after your grandfather there have been no more Grand Dukes."

"Mama cried when she read that in the newspapers," Lucia said, "but actually there was no direct heir because she had no brother."

"That is what I thought I would remember," the Marquis said, "and so, my darling, our story is quite simple."

"H-how? What are you . . . saying?"

"You are the last remaining member of the family," the Marquis said, "and just before Napoleon started to march on your country when he was gobbling up all the other small Principalities and States of Europe, you were sent to Venice to live with friends, where you have been ever since."

Lucia looked at him wide-eyed, and he went on:

"I doubt if anybody will be particularly curious and certainly not at all knowledgeable about Princess Lucia of Valenstein."

"Princess!" Lucia exclaimed.

"A title which," the Marquis went on, "as your mother's daughter, is yours, and which will be entirely acceptable to my family, who as you suspected are extremely snobbish about whom I marry."

"And you really ... think they would ... believe that?"

"And can they question it," the Marquis asked, "if I tell them the story myself?"

He smiled before he added:

"I assure you that my relatives are, on the whole, I think, rather frightened of me, and that is how we will keep them."

Lucia laughed.

"It would certainly be a tale of 'from rags to riches' and very much ... a fairy-story."

"How could it be anything else when your father and mother were so clever in getting what they wanted? And we must do the same!"

Lucia looked up at him as she asked:

"Are you really ... saying it will not ... hurt you and it will be quit ... all right for me to ... marry you?"

"I am going to marry you," the Marquis replied, "and, my darling, if your father and mother could do anything so brave as running away together in such circumstances, how can we not be just as clever in getting away with our story, which incidentally is far more creditable."

"I love you!" Lucia cried. "I love you, I love you! As I

have already said, I will . . . do anything you . . . want me to do."

Then it was impossible to say any more, for the Marquis was kissing her passionately, possessively, and the sunshine came through the mist over the horizon and enveloped them in a blaze of light.

* * *

Lucia stood in her cabin looking at herself in the mirror and thinking that what she was seeing could only be part of a dream.

It seemed as if it was only yesterday that she had been hungry and frightened when she had left the attic in which her father was so ill to go early in the morning in search of food, and instead found the Marquis in the Piazza San Marco.

"How could I have guessed . . . how could I have known for one moment that I would become his . . . wife?" she asked her reflection.

She knew now that God and her mother had been looking after her, guiding and helping her, and she had been very foolish not to realise it.

But still she could not forget how frightened she had been of her father dying and of being left alone.

Then when she had found the Marquis, everything had changed, and now seeing herself in her wedding-gown in the reflection in the mirror, she thought that she might have stepped out of one of her father's paintings.

The sunshine coming through the port-holes glittered on her hair and on the wreath of orange-blossom which covered the veil that was so fine it seemed it might have been made by fairy-fingers.

The Marquis had bought it for her at the same time that he had provided her with a number of gowns brought to the yacht by the smartest and best dressmaker in Nice.

"I have always wanted to see your beauty framed as it should be," he said, "and I have lain awake imagining you in the sort of gowns I can now give you without your being proud and refusing them."

Lucia laughed.

"How do you know I would have refused them?"

He smiled and turned her face up to his.

"I know everything about you, my darling," he said, "and I love your pride, just as I love everything else about you, because it is an intrinsic part of your character."

"If you had offered me gowns, I hope I would have been . . . correct in refusing them."

Even as she spoke she knew that because she loved him and wanted to look beautiful for him, it had been very hard not to allow him to give her anything he wanted to.

"As my wife, I want you to dazzle everybody you meet," he said. "Besides, how can a Princess be dressed as anything but a Queen?"

She laughed and said:

"I think you are calling me a Princess not only to save your face but because at heart like your relatives and all English people you are a snob!"

"I admit there is some truth in that," the Marquis said, "but, darling, whether you are a Princess by right or not, you look like one, and when you are gowned as you should be, no-one will question for a moment that you have Royal blood in your veins."

He kissed her as he spoke, and she had no chance to reply.

But now she thought that her mother would be very thrilled that after all the years of hiding and being a nobody, her daughter should take the place in Society that she had once occupied.

She had sometimes said to Lucia:

"I never for one moment regret running away with your father and being the happiest person in the world! At the same time, my darling, I would like you to live as I did in a Palace, to have the finest horses to ride, and to know that the people over whom you ruled were happy and content."

She paused for a moment to add:

"They certainly used to cheer and throw flowers into the carriage whenever we drove about Valenstein."

But to Lucia, who had known only the confines of a small cottage in Little Morden, it was difficult to visualise.

Now when she had learnt from the Marquis of the many houses he owned as well as his ancestral home in Buckinghamshire, she knew that her mother would be glad that she was to live like a Princess in what, to all intents and purposes, was a Palace.

It was easy to understand that as there had been so much confusion after Napoleon's conquest of almost the whole of Europe, and the extinction of so many small countries and Principalities, no-one in England was likely to be suspicious or ask awkward questions.

When they returned to the yacht, the Marquis said:

"I know the present Duke of Beauhampton, who, I suppose, is your uncle. It will be interesting to see when we meet him if there is any resemblance to your father."

"It is fortunate that except that I am fair, I do not very closely resemble Papa."

"I was always certain that you were not entirely English," the Marquis said, "and because you were so evasive about it, I was suspicious when you kept insisting that you were."

He put his arms round her and added:

"You are not a very good liar, my darling, and you must promise that never again will you lie to me."

"I promise you faithfully," Lucia replied, "because I have no wish ever to lie to you or tell you . . . anything but what is . . . absolutely true."

The Marquis kissed her before he said:

"Your eyes are very lovely, and I know because we are so closely attuned to each other that I will always know what is true and what is untrue."

Now as she turned away from the mirror, Lucia thought that the truth was very simple: she loved the Marquis, and when they were married she would dedicate her whole life to making him happy.

'He saved me, and he has given me so much,' she thought, 'that I cannot begin to express my gratitude except by adoring him and worshipping him for the rest of my life.'

There was a knock at the door, and when she said: "Come in!" Evans stood there.

"'Is Lordship's askin' if you're ready, Miss," he said. "'E's waiting for you in the Saloon, and the carriage's on the quay."

"I am ready," Lucia said. "Is my gown all right?"

"You looks real beautiful," Evans replied, "and that's a fact!"

There was a note of admiration in his voice that could not be anything but sincere, and Lucia smiled as she walked across the cabin.

The Marquis had already told her that when he had informed Evans they were to be married, thinking that perhaps his valet might resent it, he had said:

"That's good news, M'Lord! If you'd 'ave asked me to choose Your Lordship a wife, I couldn't 'ave found you anyone better than Miss Beaumont. She's a real Lady, even if her father were a poor artist."

Because he thought it best to have Evans telling the story they wanted everybody to know, the Marquis had then told him who Lucia was, and that it was only because her father had lost so much money in the war that he had been forced to paint under an assumed name.

"I think, Evans," he finished, "it would be wise to forget the circumstances in which we found Miss Beaumont, and I look to you to say nothing about it when we return to England."

He paused before he added:

"I am not marrying 'Miss Beaumont' but Princess Lucia of Valenstein, and that is how our marriage will be reported in the London newspapers."

As he spoke, he knew that because Evans was so devoted to him, he would be pleased to have been taken into his confidence and trusted to tell the right story to his servants in England.

He had already remembered a few more details of what had happened to Valenstein at the hands of Napoleon's Armies, and he was certain that Evans would make a good tale of it.

When Lucia joined him in the Saloon, he thought that no-one could look more like a real Princess or, better still, a Princess in a fairy-tale.

He looked at her for a long moment, then he took her hand in his and kissed it.

"I love you!" he said. "And I will be able to tell you how much and how deeply after we are married."

She blushed at the deep note in his words and the look in his eyes.

Then she preceded him down the gang-plank and into the closed carriage that was standing on the quay.

The Marquis had arranged everything, and they drove first to the *Mairie,* where under French Law they had to be married by the Mayor.

As soon as his somewhat verbose congratulations were finished, they drove from there to the English Church where a Parson was waiting for them.

The altar and the whole Church was decorated with white lilies, and as they entered there was the soft music of an organ, and the Captain and First Mate from the yacht were waiting to act as witnesses.

Otherwise the Church was empty, although to Lucia it seemed filled with the voices of angels, and she was quite certain that her father and mother were there to see her married to the man she loved.

'Only they will understand how wonderful it is to have found the one person in the whole world to whom I belong,' Lucia thought.

She was sure that just as her mother had seen her father enveloped with light, the same light was shining from her and the Marquis.

147

They vibrated to each other, and their love was as brilliant and as beautiful as the light her father had painted in his pictures.

When the Marquis put the ring on her finger, she felt herself tremble because he was touching her, and their love seemed to bring them both very close to the Divine.

"We are blessed by God," Lucia said to herself, and knew without words that the Marquis felt the same.

They signed the Register, then walked down the aisle to where the carriage was waiting for them, and when they got into it and drove off, the Marquis took her hand and raised it to his lips.

She did not speak, because she felt her whole heart and soul was still swept up into the sacred solemnity which had been part of the Wedding Service.

As if the Marquis felt the same, having kissed her hand, he drew her a little closer to him, but they drove in silence.

Only when they had travelled quite a long way did Lucia realise they were not returning to the harbour where the yacht was moored.

She looked at the Marquis for an explanation, and he said:

"I have a surprise for you, my lovely wife!"

"What is it?"

"I have not told you before that I own a Villa just outside Nice."

"Why did you keep it a secret?"

"I have not been there for several years, and I wanted to be quite certain that it was comfortable and beautiful enough for my bride and our honeymoon."

Lucia moved even closer to him to put her head on his shoulder as she said:

"Anywhere we spend our honeymoon will be . . . wonderful with you . . . but perhaps it will be even more marvellous to be in a Villa with mimosa trees and flowers everywhere I look."

"That is what I thought," the Marquis said, "and,

darling, what is more important, we can be completely alone and undisturbed there, better even than if we were on the yacht."

The horses were climbing up a steep slope, and now when they turned off the road there was a drive between high cypress trees.

At the end there was a large Villa gleaming white in the sunshine and looking like a Grecian Temple, standing high above the sea in a garden vivid with flowers and blossom.

However, it was difficult to look at anything except love in the Marquis's eyes as he drew Lucia from the carriage and through a porticoed door into a large, cool, white room that might have stepped, like her gown, out of a fairy-story.

She was to find later that the Villa was exquisitely furnished, with paintings that would have delighted her father and with views from every window that were breath-taking.

But for the moment she could see nothing but the Marquis's eyes, and they seemed to fill the whole world.

He looked at her for a long moment before he said:

"I never imagined anyone could look so lovely or so perfect! How could I be so incredibly lucky as to have found you?"

"That is what I keep asking...myself."

She thought he would kiss her, but instead he put out his hand to touch her chin, outlining it with his fingers and giving her as he did so a strange feeling, as if she were touched by the sun.

Then very gently, as if there was no hurry, he took the wreath from her head and after it the wedding-veil.

He threw them down on a chair, then again slowly and gently he pulled her into his arms and kissed her as if the touch of her lips was something he wished to savour and remember.

As always when the Marquis kissed her, she felt her whole being respond and surrender itself to him.

149

But now it was more poignant, more intense, because, incredible though it seemed, she was his wife. She bore his name and she was his.

He drew her closer and closer, then his kiss changed from being gentle to possessive, although at the same time it was reverent. She felt the fire burning on his lips, and it lit a fire within herself.

As the flames leapt higher and higher, the Marquis drew her from the room in which they were standing.

Hardly realising it was happening, Lucia found herself in a room in which there was a bed with a headboard shaped like a silver cockle-shell and a cover of exquisite lace over white satin.

The walls of the room were white too, and as she looked at them she saw with astonishment that the paintings on them were her father's.

Only the Marquis, she thought, could have thought of anything that would give her such pleasure as to become his wife with her father, as it were, blessing them with his genius.

The white walls, the beauty of the room, and the flowers that were everywhere, all seemed a fitting background not only for their love but for the light which her father had painted, and which now made Venice part of their love.

The Marquis was watching her as she looked round. Then she said:

"Oh, darling, how can I thank you once again for understanding . . . for being so . . . wonderful and so . . . different from any . . . other man in the . . . world?"

"I will tell you how you can thank me," the Marquis said. "And, my precious, I feel as if I have waited a century for your thanks."

He swept her into his arms and once again he was kissing her, but now passionately, demandingly, possessively, and as his kisses grew more intense, something wild and wonderful leapt within Lucia to respond to him.

He kissed her until the white bedroom and the

flowers both inside and outside the Villa and the sunshine whirled round them.

The sky and the whole world had disappeared, and once again there was nothing but themselves, floating into an eternity where there was only love.

Afterwards, Lucia could never remember how it had happened, but somehow she had lost her wedding-gown and was lying in the softness of the bed, and as the sun shining through the windows seemed to blind her eyes, the Marquis joined her and she was no longer alone.

"I love you, my perfect, adorable little wife!" he said. "And now at last I can tell you how much I need and want you, and how much you mean to me."

"I . . . love you . . . and there are no . . . other words but those to express what I . . . feel."

"It is what I want you to say, over and over again, so that I will believe you," the Marquis said, "because, my precious, I am still half-afraid you may vanish and I will never find you again."

"I will . . . never do that," Lucia whispered, "for without you I would . . . not only be . . . alone . . . but in darkness."

He understood what she was saying and pulled her closer still.

"The future for us both is filled with love and happiness," he said. "Never again, my beautiful wife, shall you cry or be afraid."

"I . . . I . . . love you!"

Then, because words were unnecessary, the Marquis was kissing her lips with a fire that seemed to burn into her very heart.

Then as she quivered against him, he kissed her eyes, her lips, her neck, her breasts, and as he did so she felt once again that the angels were singing overhead.

As he made her his, there was only the blazing light of love which was theirs for eternity and which came from God and was life itself.

ABOUT THE AUTHOR

BARBARA CARTLAND, the world's most famous romantic novelist, who is also an historian, playwright, lecturer, political speaker and television personality, has now written over 350 books and sold over 350 million books throughout the world.

She has also had many historical works published and has written four autobiographies as well as the biographies of her mother and that of her brother, Ronald Cartland, who was the first Member of Parliament to be killed in World War II. This book has a preface by Sir Winston Churchill and has just been republished with an introduction by Sir Arthur Bryant.

Love at the Helm, a novel written with the help and inspiration of the late Earl Mountbatten of Burma, Uncle of His Royal Highness Prince Philip, is being sold for the Mountbatten Memorial Trust.

In 1978, Miss Cartland sang an Album of Love Songs with the Royal Philharmonic Orchestra.

In 1976, by writing twenty-one books, she broke the world record and has continued for the following five years with 24, 20, 23, 24, and 24. She is in the *Guinness Book of World Records* as the currently top-selling authoress in the world.

She is unique in that she was #1 and #2 in the Dalton List of Bestsellers, and one week had four books in the top twenty.

In private life Barbara Cartland, who is a Dame of the Order of St. John of Jerusalem, Chairman of the St. John Council in Hertfordshire and Deputy President of the St. John Ambulance Brigade, has also fought for better conditions and salaries for midwives and nurses.

Barbara Cartland is deeply interested in vitamin therapy and is President of the British National Association for Health. Her book, *The Magic of Honey*, has sold throughout the world and is translated into many languages.

Her designs, *Decorating with Love*, are being sold all over the USA and the National Home Fashions League made her "Woman of Achievement" in 1981.

Barbara Cartland Romances (book of cartoons) has just been published and seventy-five newspapers in the United States and several countries in Europe carry the strip cartoons of her novels.

Barbara Cartland

The world's bestselling author of romantic fiction. Her stories are always captivating tales of intrigue, adventure and love.

☐ 23194	LOVE AND LUCIA #171	$2.25
☐ 23192	JOURNEY TO A STAR #170	$2.25
☐ 23191	A KING IN LOVE #169	$2.25
☐ 23245	THE DUKE COMES HOME #168	$2.25
☐ 23162	LOVE ON THE WIND #167	$2.25
☐ 23161	FROM HATE TO LOVE #166	$2.25
☐ 22918	A MARRIAGE MADE IN HEAVEN #165	$2.25
☐ 20307	PURE AND UNTOUCHED #164	$2.25
☐ 22916	LOVE AT THE HELM #163	$2.25
☐ 22822	WISH FOR LOVE #160	$2.25
☐ 22876	MISSION TO MONTE CARLO #161	$2.25
☐ 20574	LOOKING FOR LOVE #152	$1.95
☐ 20505	SECRET HARBOUR #151	$1.95
☐ 20235	LOVE WINS #150	$1.95
☐ 20234	SHAFT OF SUNLIGHT #149	$1.95
☐ 20126	AN INNOCENT IN RUSSIA #148	$1.95
☐ 20014	GIFT OF THE GODS #147	$1.95
☐ 20013	RIVER OF LOVE #146	$1.95
☐ 14922	A PORTRAIT OF LOVE #145	$1.95

Buy them at your local bookstore or use this handy coupon for ordering:

Bantam Books, Inc., Dept. BC2, 414 East Golf Road, Des Plaines, Ill. 60016

Please send me the books I have checked above. I am enclosing $_____ (please add $1.25 to cover postage and handling). Send check or money order —no cash or C.O.D.'s please.

Mr/Mrs/Miss_____

Address_____

City_____ State/Zip_____

BC2—3/83

Please allow four to six weeks for delivery. This offer expires 9/83.

Barbara Cartland's Library of Love

The World's Great Stories of Romance Specially Abridged by Barbara Cartland For Today's Readers.

☐ 20953   **LOVE'S HOUR** by Elinor Glyn $2.50

☐ 20500   **LOVE IN A MIST** by Pamela Wynne $2.50

Buy them at your local bookstore or use this handy coupon for ordering:

Bantam Books, Inc., Dept. BC, 414 East Golf Road, Des Plaines, Ill. 60016

Please send me the books I have checked above. I am enclosing $_____
(please add $1.25 to cover postage and handling). Send check or money order
—no cash or C.O.D.'s please.

Mr/Mrs/Miss_____

Address_____

City_____ State/Zip_____

                                                                    BC—3/83
Please allow four to six weeks for delivery. This offer expires 9/83.